Ellie's Deli

WISHING ON MATZO BALL SOUP!

Andrews McMeel Publishing
a division of Andrews McMeel Universal
1130 Walnut Street, Kansas City, Missouri 64106

www.andrewsmcmeel.com

23 24 25 26 27 SDB 10 9 8 7 6 5 4 3 2 1

Paperback ISBN: 978-1-5248-8111-5
Hardcover ISBN: 978-1-5248-8455-0

Library of Congress Control Number: 2023931849

Made by:
RR Donnelley (Guangdong) Printing Solutions Company Ltd
Address and location of manufacturer:
No. 2, Minzhu Road, Daning, Humen Town,
Dongguan City, Guangdong Province, China 523930
1st Printing – 4/10/23

Editor: Erinn Pascal
Designer: Brittany Lee
Production Editor: Dave Shaw
Production Manager: Chuck Harper

WISHING ON MATZO BALL SOUP!

BY
LISA GREENWALD

ILLUSTRATED BY
GALIA BERNSTEIN

Andrews McMeel
PUBLISHING®

K'NAIDLACH (MATZO BALLS)
always double the recipe

INGREDIENTS
2 tablespoons oil
2 eggs lightly beaten
½ cup matzo meal
½ tablespoon salt
2 tablespoons water

INSTRUCTIONS
1. Using a fork, combine the oil and eggs in a mixing bowl. Add the matzo meal and salt and blend well. Stir in the water, cover, and chill overnight. (The longer the better.)
2. Shape the mixture with wet hands, into plum-size balls tossing only once. Drop into boiling salted water. Leave stove on high. They will grow in the water. Simmer 30 to 40 minutes and serve in the soup. Makes about 16 K'naidlach.

ALWAYS have adult supervision when cooking! Make sure that the adults are handling sharp knives and other tricky kitchen supplies, like food processors. Tie any loose hair back, too. And always wash your hands with soap and water before cooking.

Chapter 1

When you accidentally overhear that your family deli is most likely going out of business, and you'll probably need to move out of the house you've lived in your whole life, there's only one thing to do.

Make a wish on chicken soup.

I know it sounds strange but it's true. I don't have any intention of stopping because it works. I know it works because right before school started this year, I wished on a  perfect pot of simmering soup that my best friend Ava and I would be in most of the same classes. And guess what? We are! It also worked the time in third grade when I wished I'd lose the top side tooth that had been wiggling for two weeks. And it worked the time in fourth grade when I wished for a snow day (even though there was no mention of snow in the forecast) so our spelling test would be postponed.

The thing is, it's not like I can just wish on any random soup at any old restaurant. I can't make wishes on lobster bisque, or corn chowder, or even the creamiest tomato soup that goes with an ooey-gooey grilled cheese sandwich.

No. I can only make wishes on one specific soup: the best chicken soup in the world at the best deli in the world—the one my family has owned for four generations.

Lukshen Deli, it's called, officially. But sometimes my family calls it Ellie's Deli because in kindergarten for show-and-tell, I brought in a picture of me in front of it, and the whole time I talked about the deli and how much I loved it, especially the pickles and the chicken soup, the crinkle-cut fries and the way the brisket smells when it's in the oven. I went on and on about all of that for so long that when kids from my class went to Lukshen, they'd tell their parents, "Oh, this is Ellie's Deli."

On the surface, Lukshen Deli is a boring brick building with white, square tables inside and a back garden where sunflowers grow in the summer. Of course it has a fryer and a walk-in freezer, a grill and to-go items like bottled soda and bags of potato chips, but it's way more than that.

It's comfort and community and family and food.

I know it's just a deli and delis don't have feelings or emotions, but to me Lukshen is like my seventh immediate family member.

There's Bubbie, Zeyda, Mom, Dad, Anna, Mabel, and then Lukshen. That's how much our deli means to me: family member status.

Lukshen means "noodle" in Yiddish, my most favorite language. Yiddish is a language that Jews in Europe used to speak a lot, and some of them still do. It's like a mixture of German and Hebrew. It's my favorite because everything in Yiddish just sounds cooler than it does in English, like somehow it manages to capture the essence of each and every word. I mean, take the word *schvitz* for example. That means "to sweat." But *schvitz* just sounds better and more accurate, doesn't it?

I'm alone in the front of the deli right now, waiting for just the exact moment when the soup begins to simmer. That's when the magic happens. That's the time to make the wish.

Please please please don't let Lukshen close. I stare deep into the soup. *Please also keep Bubbie and Zeyda healthy and alive until they're at least one hundred and twenty. Thank you, masterful brothy powers. Thank you so much.*

"Ellie?"

I whip around and see my mom looking over at me. I'm not exactly sure where she was before this, or where she came from.

"You okay?"

I clear my throat. "Yup. Fine. All good. Was just checking on the soup."

She nods like she doesn't believe me. It's kind of shocking she's never seen me do this before; it's been a few years now, but I guess I'm pretty good at keeping secrets.

It's not like I could tell her that in second grade, when I was really panicked that I would get stuck in the bathroom during a fire drill, I wished over the soup to keep it from happening. And when it worked, I kept wishing on the soup because it obviously had magical powers.

Sometimes things start and you don't expect them to keep going forever, but then then they kind of do.

"I just can't believe this, Mara. Back in the day, there'd be a line of customers by now, out the door, around the block, all waiting patiently to place their orders," Bubbie says, coming out of the back office, talking to my mom like they are in the middle of a conversation. "Sometimes not so patiently, I must add."

My mom sighs. "Mah, please, enough with the *back in the day*. I can't hear it anymore." She walks toward the back and leaves the deli, maybe to go sit in the garden for a moment. She closes the door on her way out. It's not a slam really, more of a forceful closure. I probably shouldn't read into things like this, but I do. The way my mom closes a door really says so much about her mood.

"Oh, Ellie, my doll," Bubbie says, starting to mix a bowl of matzo ball concoction. I say a quick goodbye in my head to the magical soup and I walk over to one of the smaller tables to try to finish my math homework. "This deli is my pride and joy—other than you and your sisters of course—but we need customers! Where are the customers?"

She laughs her deep, throaty laugh even though what she's saying doesn't strike me as funny.

I look up from my worksheet of word problems. "Ummm." I don't even know why I'm trying to respond to this. I clearly don't have an answer.

It's been three days since I heard Bubbie, Zeyda, Mom, and Dad having a "talk" in the den. They asked Anna, Mabel, and me to go play outside, so we knew something was up since the three of us don't really play outside all together anymore. I kind of wish we still played outside. Our swing set with the tree house looks lonely to me now.

We pretended to leave, but then we sort of just stood by the open window and listened to them talk about closing, going out of business, how we'd be able to afford our lives, the possibility of selling both houses, moving somewhere less expensive.

It was the worst conversation I've ever overheard, and I eavesdrop A LOT.

My older sister, Anna, just got her driver's license. She's coming to pick me up in a little while since Mom decided to keep the deli open late for all the Rosh Hashanah orders that she thought would be coming in. But there aren't that many coming in, which is surprising since it's the Jewish New Year and a huge holiday for us, when families all get together to eat and celebrate.

It's been this way for the past few years, though. Fewer and fewer orders for Jewish holidays. Mostly last-minute ones, smaller ones, not the hustle and bustle the way it used to be. And fewer and fewer people eating in the restaurant, too.

Everyone says it's because the Jewish community in Marlborough Lake has gotten smaller over the years. I guess that's true, but non-Jews like deli food, too, of course. I mean, how could you not like deli food? If you're vegetarian, we have amazing vegetarian stuffed peppers, and even I, someone who doesn't like peppers at all, think they're delicious.

"I'm going home, doll, no need to stay late," my Bubbie says, taking off her apron. "Tell your mother."

"Okay, Bub. Love you."

"Love you more," she replies, the way she always does.

Sometimes I think Bubbie is the one person in the world who really gets me. Like there's a certain way she looks at me, and it's almost as if she's staring right into my thoughts. One time at the end of third grade, we were all standing around after our end-of-year celebration, sort of a graduation ceremony thing. And I was so sad because I'd never have Ms. Lerner again, and Bubbie put her hand on my shoulder, and she looked at me, and I looked at her, and she pulled me into a hug because she knew without me even saying anything that I was about to cry.

BUBBIE IS THE BEST!

It's weird to think of your grandmother as your best friend and maybe soulmate, but I can't deny it—Bubbie is that person for me.

My mom comes out of the office a little later; her glasses are perched on the top of her head. "How's homework going? Anna just texted that she's on her way."

"It's good. Almost done." I look up at my mom and smile. I want to think of something comforting to say, something reassuring, but nothing comes to me.

"When you get home, please move the laundry from the washer to the dryer. Dad needs to leave for a temple board meeting, and he just put the wash in. I'd ask Mabel, but ya know . . ."

We both start laughing.

Mabel is my little sister. She's seven and the baby of the family, and nobody ever asks her to do anything. So much so that it's now become kind of a running joke. I made my mom promise that when Mabel turns eight in January, she's going to start asking her to do stuff, like emptying the dishwasher or dumping the bathroom trash into the main trash before Anna and I have to take it out. I really hope she keeps her promise.

We hear Anna honk the horn from outside and my mom shakes her head. I gather my stuff and walk outside.

Anna's in the driver's seat of my dad's old Jeep and she has her sunglasses on even though it's not even sunny anymore.

She thinks she's the coolest human in the world, but she's not, not at all.

"Ellie. Get in. Hurry up," she says, looking at her phone for a second, which is okay, I guess, since we're parked.

"Hi to you, too."

"Hi," she groans. "Can I just say something?" She turns down the music and starts driving.

"Uh-huh."

"Can you please not take the bus to Lukshen every single day and go home instead? It's so annoying that I have to come pick you up," she says.

I raise my eyebrows. "Like you don't enjoy driving all over town, Anna? Come on. I know you love it. So, stop."

"I do enjoy it, but I'm not your chauffeur. And Dad's mad about how much money I'm spending on gas lately," she answers. "Also, you don't need to hang out there all the time. It's weird. Find a hobby."

"This is my hobby. I'm interested in business ownership, and I want to take over the deli when I'm older and Bubbie and Zeyda retire."

We're at a stoplight and Anna finally turns her head to look at me. "Um, El. I don't really want to be the one to spell this out, but you know what we overheard the other day . . ."

I shake my head. "You are the most negative person ever to live, Anna."

"I'm the most realistic person ever to live, Ellie," she says, mocking me.

"You can be realistic and optimistic at the same time," I tell her, and she ignores me.

We sit there quietly for the rest of the ride and Anna blasts some angry love song, probably thinking it's cool or alternative or whatever, I don't know. My older sister is a complete mystery in some ways, but she annoys me too much now to really want to figure it out. It wasn't always like this, but somehow this is how I think it'll be from now on between us.

We get home and Mabel is sprawled across the couch eating a gigantic bowl of popcorn.

"Hey Mabes," I say. She doesn't look up from her show. "Hello! Earth to Mabel J. Glantz."

She raises a hand up in the air in sort of a backward wave.

Some people think I'm so lucky to have two sisters, but with these two, I'm not so sure. Anna is rude and negative, and Mabel is in her own little seven-year-old world.

I'm stuck in the middle like a kayaker lost at sea, bouncing from one tiny island to another tiny island, never feeling like I'm in the right place.

"Hello, my favorites," Dad says, coming down the stairs. "I'm off to a temple board meeting. Someone please move the laundry from washer to dryer."

"Mom already asked me," I groan from the armchair in the corner of the den.

"Thank you, Ellie," Dad says. He walks over and scoops me into a sideways hug. "I can always count on you."

I'm pretty sure I'm the only Glantz sister that people can count on. Some days I'm proud of that. Other days, not so much.

"Okay, I'm leaving," Dad calls out to the house. "Can we please work on turning off some of the lights? We need to conserve some energy!"

"Uh-huh," Mabel calls back. "I like the dark better, actually. It's spooky!"

A little while later, I'm moving the laundry from the washer, while Anna yells at someone over FaceTime—some boy in her class who said something rude to Anna's best friend, Phoebe. We've only been in school, like, five days and Anna's already in the middle of some drama.

Ava, my next-door neighbor and BFF since preschool, comes bursting through our front door carrying a gigantic suitcase. Since we turned eleven, we're allowed to go back and forth to each other's houses pretty much whenever we want, from 8:30 a.m. to 8:30 p.m. That's the one rule.

"Um, Aves, are you moving in?" I giggle. "What's up?"

"My mom wants me to collect any clothes you're giving away for the clothing drive," she says, almost out of

breath, plopping herself down the couch. "Why we need to do it right now, I have no idea. But yeah. Do you have any clothes?"

I think for a minute. "Yeah, down in the basement there are a few bags, actually. You know, my mom is always going through stuff and then she never actually gets around to bringing the bags to the donation bins."

Ava gives me a bewildered sort of face and goes down to the basement.

When she returns, she sits down on the couch next me. "Is Anna literally always in a fight with someone or does it just seem that way?" Ava whispers.

"I think she kinda is. Wanna come upstairs for a minute?"

Ava looks at her watch, a sparkly pink plastic one she got on a beach vacation last summer. "Yeah, for a few minutes, but it's almost eight thirty."

When we get to my room, I lie back on my bed. It feels like I've been going nonstop since seven in the morning, which I guess I kind of have.

"You okay, Ellie?" Ava asks, sitting down next to me.

"I'm so, so tired," I reply, staring up at the ceiling, wondering if I should just go to bed for the night.

"I can't believe it about the deli," Ava says. "My mom can't believe it either. I mean, no one can. My grandma is the most shocked of all."

I sit up, finally, and I watch her face fall. "What are you talking about?"

I didn't tell her, so if Ava knows about the deli closing, it must be really official, spread around the community in a way where everyone is talking about it. Does that mean it's too late to step in and try to change things? Have my soup wishes been for nothing? Maybe the magic has worn off.

"Nothing, never mind. I gotta go."

She gets up to leave and I put a hand on her shoulder.

"Ava Naomi Milkin. Tell me this instant what you've heard."

She stares at me, her green eyes as wide as I've ever seen them. "I heard the deli is gonna close," she says, so quiet it's pretty much a whisper. "I thought you knew."

"I didn't know it was official, like one hundred percent definitely happening," I say so quietly, it's practically a whisper.

Ava is a master eavesdropper, like me, but sometimes she gets confused.

This deli decision is not definite yet. I know it's not, because my parents haven't officially told us.

I HOPE

So that means there's still time.

Still time for my soup wishes to work.

Still time to save my deli.

CHICKEN SOUP

Note from author: This came from my own Bubbie's secret recipes, and it's written exactly as she shared it with my mom. Now it's shared with you!

INGREDIENTS

4 pounds of chicken

    (try to use dark meat chicken legs and second joints for strong

    soup, but don't worry if you use whole chickens, it will still be good)

At least 4 quarts of water

Carrots, celery, onion, parsley, and dill

    (as much as or as little as you want)

Salt, pepper, onion powder, and garlic powder, to taste

INSTRUCTIONS

1. Skin the chicken and remove all fat.

2. Place the chicken in two pots and cover with cold water and some salt.

3. Bring to a boil. Lower the heat and keep skimming white foam off of the chicken until there is no more.

4. Cover the pots and cook the chicken for about an hour and 15 minutes.

5. Add some carrots, celery, onion, parsley, parsley root, and dill to the pots and cook and cook and cook. You may need to add some water as it cooks.

INSTRUCTIONS CONTINUED

6. After a while, add seasoning to taste. A little salt, pepper, onion powder, and garlic powder. Do it lightly because you can always add more but you can't subtract.

7. Cook 3 to 4 hours or until it tastes good to you. As I said, you may have to add water as it cooks.

8. When you think it is done, cool it. Strain the vegetables and combine both pots of soup. If one is lacking something, the other will make up for it.

9. Have chicken for dinner, then chicken salad for lunch the next day. Freeze some chicken because there will be a lot.

10. It is really simple, just time-consuming, but very rewarding when your grandchildren say you make the best chicken soup.

Chapter 2

The next morning, I brush my teeth, get dressed, and hurry downstairs. I realize I never saw my parents last night because I fell asleep early, and Dad was at the temple meeting late. I guess Mom was working on stuff at the deli pretty late, too.

Anna and Mabel are already eating breakfast—cereal with cut-up banana—and soon we'll all head to our different schools. I'll have to make it through the whole day without knowing what's going on with the deli.

It feels impossible.

My mom is sitting at the table with Anna and Mabel, on her laptop. I stare at her so intensely that maybe she'll feel my gaze and look up and then we can make eye contact and I can ask her.

But after a minute or two, I can't take it anymore.

"Mom," I say.

She looks up.

"Can I talk to you?"

"El, I'm kind of in the middle of something," she says in her tired voice.

"I really need to talk to you," I say firmly, not trying to worry her but also trying to worry her just the littlest bit so she pays attention. "Come with me into the den."

She's reluctant but stands up and we go to the den.

"I'm just gonna come out and say this," I say with my arms folded across my chest. "I mean, ask this. Um. Okay. First of all, it's weird you were at the deli so late last night, when we barely had any customers. And second of all—is the deli definitely closing?"

Mom's eyes crinkle a bit. She doesn't answer.

"Mom? Hello? Did you hear me?"

"We're considering closing, yes." Mom sighs, looking at the floor. "We're losing more money than we are taking in. It's costing us a lot to stay open."

I pause. "So, like, is this definite?"

"I don't know, Ellie," she says, exasperated. "Now isn't the time to have this conversation. Please get your stuff and go to the bus. Okay? I love you."

"Fine," I groan, about to ask if what I overheard was true—that if the deli closes, we'll have to sell the house and move somewhere more affordable—but I don't. The words don't come out, even though it feels like they're on the tip of my tongue. "Love you too."

So that was definitely not successful. But that's okay. It was a first try, really, and first tries are rarely successful.

Lucky for me, Ava is my best friend and next-door neighbor, so we basically do everything together, including taking the bus to school.

She meets me on the one square of sidewalk between her house and ours, and we start walking together.

"Sorry I freaked you out last night," she whispers.

"It's okay," I whisper back. "I mean, it's not okay, but it is. You know what I mean."

We giggle for a second because even though I'm not making any sense at all, she does know what I mean, and I'm thankful for that!

In a world where I feel like so few people understand me, Ava is someone who does. That's pretty huge.

"My mom says it's because the Jewish community in Marlborough Lake is getting smaller," Ava says. I want to run back to my house and bury my head under my pillow. I can't take this negativity so early in the morning. And I don't know why Ava's mom always has these grown-up conversations with her. Maybe because Ava's an only child, so her mom thinks of her as an adult.

I mean, she's right about the Jewish community, of course, and we all know it, but she doesn't have to be so blunt about it.

"Uh-huh," I reply, hoping she'll get the hint that I don't want to talk about it.

"You know, I think a lot of people are just moving away . . ." Ava keeps talking, clearly repeating stuff her mom told her, and I try to tune it out.

I think about my favorite black cherry soda from the deli and how I love the French fries that get extra crispy. I picture the photo of Bubbie, Zeyda, Aunt Clara, and Mom that hangs above the front door. Mom has her hair up in a high ponytail and she looks like a supermodel.

"So, there aren't as many people who want kosher food, and follow the dietary laws and stuff . . ."

"Ava." I stop in the middle of the walk to the bus. "I know you're trying to help explain things, which I usually really appreciate, but I don't want to talk about it right now."

"I'm sorry. Again."

I sigh. "I think I just don't like to give up on things. I can't give up on things. It's like, against my personal beliefs."

"Obviously," she says softly. "Definitely don't give up. We'll think of something. Come straight to my house for a brainstorm session after school."

I want to tell her about the wishes, about the magical soup, about how I can change the course of this whole thing. But I can't seem to open my mouth and come clean about it. Obviously, she'll be shocked.

"Wait," I say, realizing I need more time with the soup. "Come with me to the deli instead, we can brainstorm there!"

Ava smiles. "Done and done. I'll be there. Please text your Bubbie to have three thousand half sour pickles waiting for me."

"Done and done."

◀ 9

Bubbie

Message
Today 11:28 AM

Hi Bubbie. Ava and I are coming to Lukshen after school. Ava wants 3,000 sour pickles!! And I want 3,000 more 😊 Love you

SWEET AND SOUR MEATBALLS

INGREDIENTS
½ cup water
⅓ cup packed dark brown sugar
¼ cup lemon juice
1 tablespoon ketchup
¾ pound ground steak
1 egg
¼ cup dry breadcrumbs
¼ teaspoon salt
Dash of pepper

INSTRUCTIONS
1. About 30 minutes before serving, in a medium saucepan, combine the water, brown sugar, lemon juice, and ketchup. Heat to boiling.

2. In a medium bowl, combine the ground steak, egg, breadcrumbs, salt, and pepper.

3. Shape into about 30 small meatballs. Add to the boiling sauce.

4. Cook covered over low heat for 15 minutes.

Chapter 3

It's really hard to make it through the school day. All I want to do is get to the deli and the soup to make an extra-strong wish. It sounds funny, even inside my head, but it's how I feel.

It's a bummer all this deli stuff is happening now because we're still in the fresh, new, exciting part of the year: new notebooks, new schedules, sneakers that aren't dirty yet. September is kind of magic in that way, and I'm wasting it feeling antsy about the deli.

Ava, Aanya, Sally, Brynn, and I get to the cafeteria a few minutes early for lunch, so we're the first ones there. I slowly open my brown paper lunch bag; I'm going to need to force myself to eat this tuna sandwich. The bread looks soggy, but I'll be starving if I don't eat it.

I look over at my friend Aanya's lunch and immediately feel jealous as I see all the fresh vegetables and perfect pillowy pieces of tofu in the most

delicious-looking coconut curry sauce. She's eating restaurant food in the school cafeteria!

"Aan, that looks SO good!" I tell her.

She smiles. "It is. My mom hung out with my aunt last night, so she brought back tons of stuff from Taste of India. I think I'll be eating it all week."

"That's amazing. I think you have the best lunch in this whole cafeteria."

Aanya's cousin's family owns Taste of India downtown, a few stores away from Lukshen. I need to start bringing lunch from the deli.

I'm about to bite into my sandwich, trying not to gag, when Ms. Tarmesh, our principal, comes over to our table with a girl I don't recognize.

"Hi, girls," Ms. Tarmesh says. "I want to introduce you to a new student. She'll be joining your table for the rest of lunch today."

We all look up and smile.

Ms. Tarmesh continues, "This is Nina. She just moved here from Chicago."

I wonder why she didn't start on the first day of school.

"Hi, Nina," we say almost in unison.

"Nice to meet you," I add. "Come sit."

Ms. Tarmesh leaves and Nina sits down. She has a bright orange bottle of Vitamin Water and turkey on a roll wrapped in white paper like she just came from a fancy sandwich shop. Plus, she has beaded bracelets halfway up her left arm. She looks way older than sixth grade. I'd say maybe even eighth grade if I didn't know better.

"How do you like Marlborough Lake so far?" I ask her.

"It's cool, I mean, we moved 'cuz of my dad's job." Her voice rises at the end, like she's a little unsure. "I don't even totally understand what my dad does, though, to be honest." She fiddles with her bracelets. "It seems nice here, but I miss Chicago. I went to the same school the Obama girls went to. Kind of my claim to fame! We weren't there at the same time, but still."

"Yeah, definitely still cool," I add, and then I start to get a panicky sort of feeling—like this could be me if we lose the deli. Like I could have to move somewhere new, and scary and unknown. And I could be the girl who's brought over to a random table in an unfamiliar cafeteria.

I don't want any of that to happen.

Aanya, Sally, Brynn, and Ava ask Nina a million questions as I quietly freak out about my future. Ava, of course, wants to know if Nina has brothers or sisters since she's an only child and obsessed with siblings.

Turns out Nina has twin older sisters and they're in eighth grade.

Sally asks her about where she lives in Marlborough Lake. "Umm, I think the neighborhood is called The Sands?" Everything Nina says comes out like a question.

"Yeah, that's where I live," Aanya and Brynn answer at the same time and then high-five. "We'll show you around."

Soon, lunch ends, and we go back to class. Nina follows Sally since they're both in Mr. Kennerson's math class.

Ava and I walk together.

"She seems nice," Ava says.

"Yeah."

"What, Ellie?" She stops and glares at me. "You don't like her?"

"Huh? I never said that." I don't meet Ava's gaze.

"I can tell exactly what you're thinking at all times, Eleanor Talia Glantz. So don't try and fool me."

I crack up the way I always do when Ava and I speak to each other with our full names.

"I'm just a little freaked out because, like, Nina moved because of her parents' jobs . . . and that could be me, too. Like if the deli really does close, we won't have any money, we won't be able to stay in our house, maybe we won't even be able to stay in Marlborough Lake . . ." I stare at her. "My whole family depends on the deli! And what other jobs could my parents even do? They don't have any other skills."

I'm about to finally come clean and confess about the soup wishes, for real this time, and tell her how I'm worried but I know it'll be okay because I have the magical soup, but then Ava stares deep into my eyes and puts her hands on my shoulders like she's about to offer some kind of blessing, like the rabbi does for bar and bat mitzvah students.

"Listen, I've been thinking a lot about this, and I've been kind of scared to bring it up, but here goes . . . just because the Marlborough Lake Jewish community is dwindling, doesn't mean that Lukshen Deli has to disappear along with it . . . you won't have to move, your parents won't need new jobs . . . we can fix this."

I do a slow nod, waiting to hear what she's going to say next. "Okay . . . go on."

Sure, I have the soup, but actual plans can't hurt. I mean, the more things to try, the better!

"We need to spruce it up, make changes, sort of bring it into the current time," she says. "It feels like it's stuck in the nineties."

"What do you know about the nineties, Ava?" I giggle.

"Whatever my mom tells me, which is a lot, plus you know I've seen like every episode of *Friends,* most more than once, but anyway." She raises her eyebrows and stares at me. "Listen,

Ellie. I was going to save this for the brainstorm session this afternoon, but I'll tell you now. It's up to us to take Lukshen to the next level and bring it into the next generation. Think about it this way: Lukshen doesn't do delivery, has no social media presence, and no offense, but there's nothing cool or hip about it, and Marlborough Lake is becoming very hip."

I laugh. "It is? Is this something you overheard your mom say?"

She nods, giggling for a second behind her hands. "Um, yes, that new coffee shop with the neon tables! The sushi place with the amazing omakase special! Seriously. You need to listen to me. Don't let the deli disappear by keeping it stuck in the past. Make changes, make it cool, and get with the times, girl! Maybe we can even loop in some kind of celebrity chef, maybe there's a reality show for struggling businesses! Who even knows! Unlimited possibilities!"

"Ava!" I burst out laughing, feeling relief from all the dark things I was thinking and saying before. "You're too much. Where do you get this stuff?"

She shrugs. "No clue. Anyway, think about it, and I'll see you at the bus, and we'll go right to Lukshen and come up with ideas!"

We walk into English and my mind starts spinning, bouncing off all the things that Ava said.

She's right: no social media, no delivery, nothing fancy or hip or fun. Still the same booths and tables from back in the day, which definitely haven't been updated since Mom started working at the deli full time after college.

Our teacher, Ms. Tomasso, is going on and on about strategies for writing a book report and it's the most boring lesson I've ever sat through. She's making it seem like there's some formula or something and we all have to follow it.

That's not me. I like to do things my own way. Even when it comes to book reports.

I spend the whole lesson daydreaming about the new and improved Lukshen Deli and all the things we can do.

Maybe even write and publish a cookbook with all the recipes dating back to my great-grandmother, Bubbie's mom.

Maybe we can get live music sometimes, too, and spruce up the backyard area so people can eat outside. Maybe we can host small weddings and bar and bat mitzvahs and baby namings!

I want to do all of this. But I don't want to wait for approval from Mom or Bubbie or Zeyda.

I want to do it all right now, on my own.

If only I were twenty-five instead of eleven.

Everything would be so much easier.

BAKED STEAK

INGREDIENTS

½ teaspoon salt
1 small clove garlic
½ cup ketchup
1 teaspoon Worcestershire sauce
2 teaspoons melted margarine or oil
½ teaspoon lemon juice
1 large onion, chopped
London broil or filet mignon

INSTRUCTIONS

1. Combine the salt, garlic, ketchup, Worcestershire sauce, oil, lemon juice, and chopped onion to create a marinating sauce.

2. Marinate the meat in the sauce all day or overnight.

3. Bake in a 375 degree oven for 45 minutes or until done.

Chapter 4

On the bus to Lukshen after school, Ava talks a lot about Nina. "She's so cool, did you see how many bracelets she has?" Ava asks me.

"Yeah. I did. Very cool."

"I mean, she lived in, like, a skyscraper in Chicago. I think the elevator opened right into her living room, and now she's in a house right on the lake. I feel like everywhere she lives is so fabulous." Ava takes a breath and finally stops talking for a second.

I shrug. "Yeah, sounds like it, Aves."

"I just think it's cool we have a new girl here. We haven't had a new kid in so long, not since Derek O'Connell moved here at the end of third grade."

"True."

Ava readjusts herself so she's facing me instead of facing the back of the seat in front of her. "Are you okay, Ellie? You seem really, really out of it."

I inhale and exhale and then inhale and exhale again. "I feel really, really out of it," I admit. "I can't get out of my own thoughts."

Ava giggles. "It sounds like you're a tiny creature trapped in a giant cartoon brain."

The way she says it, it sounds hilarious and ridiculous, and soon I'm laughing so much, Ava starts laughing hysterically, too, and half the bus turns around to look at us.

It feels so good to laugh like this, almost like it's a sponge wiping away the dirt that's been lingering there, stuck, making everything feel blurry and messy.

We get to Lukshen Deli and walk around to the back so we can drop our bags in the office. Through the window, I see my mom and Bubbie slumped over a table, looking a little worn out, a stack of paper surrounding them.

"Oh, hi, dolls," Bubbie says, perking up as soon as she sees us. "Ava! How are you, darling?"

"I'm good." She smiles. "Starving."

"Well, you're in the right place!" Bubbie chuckles. She hops up from the table and goes behind the deli counter. "I'll make a spread for you girls, extra pickles! Learning all day makes you hungry! Your brains work very hard. You work very hard!"

They dive into some detailed conversation about homework and tests and how kids are too busy these days, and I sneak away, quietly, behind the counter, to the stove with the soup.

It's already simmering, a low boil, ready for any customers who come in.

This will work.

Oh, masterful brothy powers, please save Lukshen! Please help me save Lukshen. Please don't make me move away. Please help keep things the way they are, but better, the way they used to be, I guess. Maybe even better than that!

"How was everyone's day?" my mom asks.

"It was fine," Ava and I answer at the same time.

"We have a math test next week," I add.

"I'm sure you'll do great," my mom replies, looking down at the paper in front of her. It seems like she has extra wrinkles around her eyes, and the skin underneath them looks saggy.

I wish she didn't look like this. I don't want to see my mom all worn out and agitated and stressed.

Bubbie comes back with a platter of half sour pickles, some grilled vegetables, a knish for each of us, and two mini turkey sandwiches on little teeny-tiny rolls.

This is really not a snack—it's more like a full meal—but Ava and I don't complain.

My mom and Bubbie go back to the office for a conference call with other small business owners or something. To be honest, I sort of zoned out when they started talking about it.

Ava and I sit at the table and munch on our snack.

"So, what do you think the first step of our plan should be?" Ava asks me.

I crunch my pickle. "I've been thinking about this all day, and I don't even know! There's too much to do. I don't know where to even start!"

"Okay, calm down. Here's my idea," Ava starts, but she's interrupted by a plump little man bursting through the door. His hair is disheveled, and he appears to be out of breath.

"Hello? Hello! Hello?" He says the word over and over again, half like an exclamation and half like a question.

"Hello!" Ava yells back. "How can we help?"

I try not to laugh as she acts like she works here, like she's an actual Lukshen Deli employee.

"My wife is sick and pregnant and she needs chicken soup, and your line is busy!" He's sort of screaming now and looks like he might burst into tears. "Your phone has been busy for hours."

Ava and I look over toward the phone at the same time. Lukshen Deli may be the only remaining business in the world with only a landline phone. I guess it really is stuck in the past in way more ways than one.

"I'll go look into that, um," I start. "And, um, I'll go find someone who can give you as much chicken soup as you'd like. It really does have healing powers." (Ahem, wishing on soup, but I don't say that part.) "We need to get that to your wife right away."

The man stands there huffing and buffing, wiping sweat off the top of his forehead with a napkin from one of the tables.

I walk back to the office to get my mom or Bubbie.

"What can we do for you, Ellie?" my mom asks, but what she's really saying is *please don't interrupt me.*

"It's not for me, first of all," I say, and the words come out sounding harsh even though I don't really mean for them to.

"But the phone line has been busy, I guess, and there's a man here who really needs soup."

Out of the corner of my eye, I see Ava scribbling something down on a napkin. I'll have to check in on that in a second. I wait for my mom or Bubbie to respond to this man, but they seem to be taking forever.

"A man here is desperate for soup. DESPERATE FOR SOUP," I say as forcefully as I can, thinking to myself that if he only knew how magical the soup was, he'd be even more desperate for it. "He's been trying to get through on the phone and couldn't."

My mom and Bubbie glare at each other like they're secretly blaming the other one for this problem.

"Are you guys going to do something? Help? Get him some soup?" My mouth hangs open. I don't know what they're doing, what they're thinking, why they're sitting there frozen in place. I don't know what's wrong with them or what's going on.

I walk back to the front of the deli and Ava is standing there talking to the sweaty, desperate-for-soup man.

"Do you usually order delivery or pickup from places?" Ava asks, taking notes on a napkin. "Or do you usually cook?"

He hesitates a minute. "My wife cooks usually, but she's sick and I'm stressed and overwhelmed with work." He seems impatient, and then mildly relieved when he sees us walking over.

"So would a delivery option for this deli be helpful to you?" Ava asks, so seriously that it almost makes me crack up. I'm not sure who she thinks she is right now.

"It would be, yes. But please. I just need to get the soup and get home to my wife." He looks like he may cry any second.

"Hello," my mom says with a sigh, very worn-out sounding. "How can I help?"

"Soup, please. Three quarts of your famous chicken soup with matzo balls. And please fix your phones. This has been quite an ordeal," Schvitzy Man says.

"I'll get that for you right away, on the house. Again, so sorry for the hassle." My mom sighs and goes behind the counter to dole out the soup.

Ava and I make eyes at each other. *On the house?*

Not really sure they should be giving anything for free away right now, but I don't think this is the time to debate with them.

Ava and I head to the back office where we find Bubbie researching something on her laptop. When she sees us, she quickly closes it and tells us she has to take care of something in the kitchen.

I wonder what that's about. Little bubbles of tension seem to attack my stomach, like they're toppling over on each other.

Ava sits down on the spinny desk chair and takes a lip gloss out of her pocket, and then an absolutely brilliant idea (maybe the most brilliant idea I've ever had) pops into my brain!

"Oh!" I shout. "I have the best idea ever and your lip gloss made me think of it!"

"Huh?" Ava asks, rolling her lips together. "Who knew a lip gloss could be so inspiring?" She laughs.

"A loyalty thing! Like a program, you know what I mean. Like at Coco's at the mall. Remember how we earned enough points for a free lip gloss? The one you're using right now!"

"Oh! Yes!" Ava claps. "Lukshen Loyalty! Spend a certain amount and get free soup!"

"Exactly!" I scream.

Bubbie peaks into the office. I wonder if she's been listening outside this whole time. Maybe that's where I get my eavesdropping habit from . . .

"Ladies, shhh. My head."

"Sorry," we say at the same time, and then walk together toward the front because Ava's mom will be here soon to get us.

We didn't make a ton of progress today, but we made a little. And I definitely came up with an amazing idea.

It's something.

I'll take it.

MOCK CHOPPED LIVER

INGREDIENTS

1 large can green peas
2 sauteed onions
3 hard-boiled eggs
½ cup walnuts

INSTRUCTIONS

1. Put everything in a food processor until it looks pasty!

Chapter 5

*A*t school on Monday, Nina is in a one-on-one conversation with Ava about the hang-out they're having after school.

"So glad you remembered the change of clothes," Nina tells Ava like she's about to launch into a long list of instructions. "That way you're not in the clothes you wore all day. My mom hates germs, and we always change when we get home. We can walk into town from my house and go to the candy store and get whatever we want. My mom got me one of those kids debit cards." Nina pauses then, like she's waiting to see if any of us have them, too.

I don't think any of us have one of those, but it sounds pretty cool. Maybe I can convince my parents to get me one.

Ava and I walk together to class after lunch. I have a moment of gratitude that Nina isn't in any of my classes and then I have a moment of guilt that I feel this way about her.

"Are you excited to hang out with Nina?" I ask her.

"Yeah," she says, not looking at me. "Don't be jealous. I'm sure she'll ask you to come over soon, too. She hasn't asked Aanya, Brynn, or Sally yet, either."

"I'm not jealous."

We're quiet the rest of the walk to class and when we get there, everyone is silent already. I look toward the whiteboard, and it says GOALS in huge letters.

Ms. Tomasso is seated at her desk.

Ava and I sideways glance at each other, like we're unsure if we're supposed to know what's going on.

"Girls, you're late," Ms. Tomasso says. "Remember it's important to be prompt after lunch."

My throat tightens and I feel like I might burst into tears right here. It's not like we're in major trouble, but it still feels miserable.

"Take out a sheet of paper," she continues. "I want to know your goals for the year."

"Our goals?" Ava chokes out the words a little. "What do you mean? What kind of goals?"

"Goals. That's it. Whatever that means to you, Ava." Ms. Tomasso pauses. "Okay, get to it. Start writing."

I need to ask Ava if she thinks Ms. Tomasso is the meanest teacher we've ever had. I'm pretty sure she is, but I want another opinion.

I stare at the whiteboard and the word GOALS and then look back down at my blank sheet of paper. I glance around the class to see who is writing and who isn't, and it looks like everyone else is writing.

What are my goals? I don't even know. I wish we'd been warned about this so I could have maybe prepared a little.

I think a few more minutes and then I start writing.

I write about my goal of feeling more confident, more secure. I write about my goal for Lukshen and how to make sure it stays in business, how we need this family business to pay the bills but it's also a lot more than that. It's literally like another family member. We need it. It's who we are. I can't even imagine us without it.

Even though I had no ideas for this at first, once I start writing, everything flows and I feel an energy I haven't felt in a while. Like I needed more than anything to get this all down on paper even though I didn't realize it.

Maybe Ms. Tomasso isn't mean at all; maybe she's a mind reader and she knew just what I needed.

"Okay, class, time to stop. Please leave your papers on the red bin on my desk. I'm looking forward to reading them. We'll continue this throughout the year, and you'll see how your goals ebb and flow and evolve, and then in June, you'll have them all assembled into a notebook to read over, a piece for true reflection and introspection."

"She talks to us in such an official way, like we're in an office or something," Tyler Vincent says, loud enough for everyone to hear, and the whole class cracks up.

"Mr. Vincent," Ms. Tomasso says in her warning tone.

He lowers his head and stops talking. This isn't his first warning.

At the end of the day, we head to the buses, but Ava isn't going home with me since she's going to Nina's.

"I'll come over tonight and tell you all about it," she whispers.

I want to say it's okay and she doesn't have to, but I don't. I just nod. It's still pretty cool that we can go back and forth to each other's homes on our own without it being a huge deal.

The bus ride home is lonely without Ava, but I try not to think about it. Instead, I keep my brain focused on the goals thing. I wonder what goals I left out, and if they'll come to me later.

And that's when I get another incredible epiphany! A bolt of lightning of an idea that I cannot ignore, a giant light bulb over my head that energizes me in a way I've maybe never been energized before. I feel like my mind explodes with amazing ideas at the most random times lately.

A goals journal!

As soon as I get home, I'm going to beg Anna to drive me over to Marlborough Lake Stationery and buy the prettiest journal I can find. I still have some Chanukah money left over from last year and this is the perfect thing to spend it on.

This way, every day, I can write down goals I have, and I can check off what I've accomplished so it can also help me keep track of the stuff I want to do for the deli.

I run off the bus and into the house. Anna is sprawled out on the couch with her feet resting on the top.

"Hi, Anna, can I ask you the biggest favor?"

No response.

"Anna! Hi!"

No response.

I tickle the bottom of her foot and she jerks up.

"What? Ellie, ew. Stop."

"I tried to get your attention before the tickle," I explain, trying not to laugh.

"What do you want, Ellie?" she says while looking at her phone.

"Please, pretty please, can you drive me to the stationery store? I need something right away," I say.

"Who needs stationery right away?" Anna laughs. "You have an urgent letter-writing campaign coming up?"

"I need a journal. Please just take me. Mom said Mabel is going to Julia's after school, so we don't need to wait for her. Come on, please, it'll be so fast."

She stares at me for a few moments before answering. If she doesn't agree, I'll have to remind her that the whole reason she has Dad's old Jeep is because she's supposed to help out Mom and Dad by driving Mabel and me where we need to go.

"Fine. But it better be quick."

"Thank you so much." I reach out to hug her and she actually lets me.

I realize it's been so long since we've hugged or cuddled—both things we used to do all the time. Maybe Anna's changed, or maybe I've changed, or maybe both. No matter what, things changed, and I didn't even notice it or realize it until now. I want to get things back on track, or at least closer to the way they used to be.

We're quiet on the drive to Marlborough Lake Stationery, and then Anna turns to me while at a red light.

"You doing okay, El?" she asks, and the concern in her voice almost makes me burst into tears, but I manage to hold them in. I don't remember the last time she's asked me that, and it feels overwhelming but also great. Maybe there's a way for us to get back on the path to where we used to be.

"Kinda, sorta. Maybe." I shrug. "I mean, not really."

"No?" she asks, not looking at me, because we're driving again.

"I feel like everything is weird," I admit, grateful for the opportunity to open up.

"What do you mean, *everything?*"

"Well, like the deli. I'm worried about it, obviously, and how will we have money if the deli closes? I have a lot of ideas to save it, but I'm also worried no one will listen to me since I'm just a kid. And then, like, with Ava." I feel the tears ready to flood my face again, but I stop talking and focus all my energy on keeping them in. "See, there's this new girl, Nina, who moved here from Chicago, and she's so cool and she seems so much older than I am, and I think Ava's obsessed with her. She's at her house right now." I pause. "I don't know; it just feels weird that Ava suddenly has this new friend. What if she ends up liking her more than she likes me?"

Just hearing the words come out of my mouth makes my throat feel like a lumpy mountain range.

Anna nods like she's taking it all in and trying to carefully think of a response. "I know what you're saying. I've felt that way before."

Even that simple, little sentence feels good to me, reassuring, like I'm not totally alone in my thoughts because she understands them.

"Do things feel weird for you?" I ask her.

"In some ways, yeah. In other ways, no."

I wait for her to elaborate but she doesn't, and then we're quiet for the two minutes left in the drive.

"I'll wait for you in the car, okay?" she asks. "Or do you want me to come in? Do you need another opinion for your journal?"

"Yeah." I smile. "Come in, that'll be helpful!"

She turns the car off, and we walk inside. I'm not sure I realized how much I needed that little chat, but I really, really did.

We walk around Marlborough Lake Stationery. It smells like a mixture of vanilla and cinnamon and they're playing soft, soothing classical music and it sort of feels like I could stay in here forever, like it's a cozy blanket of a place.

"Ooh, what about this one?" Anna holds up a pale pink journal with gold embossed lowercase letters that spell out *notes and thoughts.*

It's perfect.

"Yes," I say. "I love it."

Anna links arms with me and we go to pay, and I'm suddenly overflowing with love for her and for this store and for this moment we shared.

Before today, I never would have guessed that buying a journal could be such a monumental experience.

Chapter 6

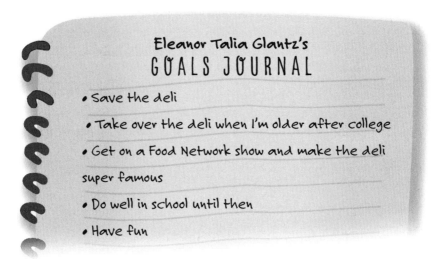

Eleanor Talia Glantz's
GOALS JOURNAL

- Save the deli
- Take over the deli when I'm older after college
- Get on a Food Network show and make the deli super famous
- Do well in school until then
- Have fun

I wait all night for Ava to come over and tell me about the hang with Nina. I organize my bookshelf, fold a whole drawer of shirts, and then fold them again.

I do a quick online search for magical soup to see if it's an actual thing that other people have encountered somehow. And then a search on different stores' loyalty programs so I can figure out how to make Lukshen Loyalty happen.

Finally, it gets to be eight o'clock and Ava still hasn't texted or come over.

I can't wait any longer. I need to go. I need to go now.

"Um, Ellie," Mabel says when I'm by the front door slipping on my sneakers with the laces still tied. "Where are you going?"

"Ava's. Be right back."

"I don't know why I even bothered to ask." Mabel shakes her head. "*Of course* you're going to Ava's."

I run down the three steps to my front walkway and then hustle next door. We've timed it and it takes me exactly one and a half minutes to get from my front door to hers.

"Hi, Ellie," Ava's mom says, opening the door. "Everything okay?"

"Yeah, Ava didn't text like she said she would, so I wanted to make sure *she* is okay," I explain.

Her mom looks confused. "She's fine. You can go upstairs."

I smile and walk inside. "Thanks."

I run upstairs to Ava's room. She's on her window seat reading a graphic novel I know for a fact she's already read three hundred times.

"You didn't text me!"

"Um, hi, Ellie." She giggles.

"Don't 'hi, Ellie' me!" I sit on the edge of her bed. "So. How was it?"

"How was what? My orthodontist appointment isn't until next week, and even so I'm not getting braces right away. I already told you that." She closes the book and looks over at me, her eyes all squinty.

"I'm not talking about braces!" I shake my head. "I'm talking about the Nina hang."

Ava bulges her eyes at me. "Um, Ellie. I thought you didn't care."

I hesitate then, because the truth is, I *also* thought I didn't care. "I'm just curious," I say softly.

Ava hops away from the window seat and sits next to me on her bed. She drapes an arm over my shoulder and leans her cheek against my cheek. For some reason, these little gestures almost make me start to cry and I choke back the tears, trying as hard as I can to get them to stay back inside my eyes.

"Ellie, what's going on? Be honest. Let it all out."

"I just feel shaky," I tell her. "Like things aren't the way they're supposed to be."

"Okay, well, we'll get things to be how they're supposed to be, I promise. The two of us together—there's literally nothing we can't do, including saving Lukshen." She pauses, and I try as hard as I can to believe her. "Anyway, the Nina hang was fine. Her house is awesome, and she has an outdoor hot tub, but we didn't go in it because I forgot my bathing suit. Anyway, it was fun and we had fun, but she's not you and she'll never be you, so stop feeling jealous."

I sniffle a little. "I'm not jealous."

"Ellie."

"Ava."

"Ellie."

We could go back and forth like this for a bit, but finally we stop and then we crack up and I fall backward on Ava's bed.

"So then why didn't you text me right away?" I ask her, still laughing a little bit.

"There wasn't that much to say about it, and I got distracted." She shrugs. "Really. I promise it wasn't all that exciting."

I nod. "Okay. I believe you. It's getting late, though, and I should probably get home." I pause. "Can you come over after school tomorrow so we can do more brainstorming?"

"Yes! And I have such a good idea. My mom's friend Terri runs the Marlborough Lake PR agency—I don't think that's the exact name, but you know what I mean. Anyway, my mom said that she's the expert with like marketing and PR strategy and stuff."

"Oh." I look down at Ava's purple carpet and rub my socked feet back and forth.

"What? Why do you look sad again?"

"'Cuz we can't afford to pay this Terri lady. She'll want to be paid."

"Maybe. Maybe not. Who knows? Maybe she'll take a shine to us since we're kids and stuff? We can write a super nice email." Ava shrugs. "We'll figure it out."

"Are you sure?"

"Yes! I'm always sure." Ava wraps me in a sideways hug. "But I need to get ready for bed now. I'm kind of shocked my mom hasn't come up here yet, wondering what's happening. She's probably listening at the door."

We're quiet for a few seconds and then Ava yells out, "Mom!" We hear footsteps tapping along the wooden floor of Ava's upstairs hallway.

"Told ya!"

We laugh because Ava was totally right.

"Okay, tomorrow, we're on." I hug her again, get up from the bed, and slip my sneakers on with my heels smooshing down the back since I'm kind of in a hurry to get home.

After I get home, I head upstairs, brush my teeth, and change into my comfiest pajamas with neon hearts. I need to be in my bed, under my covers, thinking about things quietly without distractions. I'm still twisted up about the Nina and Ava thing, like Ava will end up liking Nina so much more and I'll be left behind. And the deli, too—I mean, it's a lot to worry about all at once.

Eventually I fall asleep and dream about moving to a farm where my only job is to mow the lawn and hang out with the chickens, like talk to them and stuff and they actually talk back to me.

It's the weirdest dream ever and I have no idea what it means.

And when I wake up in the morning, I'm shocked to find myself in my bed, under my rainbow comforter in my room on Courtyard Street in Marlborough Lake.

That's how real the dream was.

I truly believed I lived on a farm and talked to chickens. Maybe it's some manifestation of the magical chicken soup thing. Maybe me talking to chickens meant that I feel disconnected from actual humans.

Could be both.

FUDGY BROWNIES

INGREDIENTS

4 squares unsweetened chocolate
½ cup butter or margarine
2 cups sugar
4 eggs, beaten
1 cup sifted flour
1 teaspoon vanilla
1 cup chopped walnuts

INSTRUCTIONS

1. Melt the chocolate and butter in a double boiler. Let cool slightly.

2. Meanwhile, gradually add the sugar to the eggs, beating thoroughly after each addition.

3. Blend in the chocolate mixture, then stir in the flour.

4. Add the vanilla and nuts.

5. Spread the mixture in a greased 9-inch square pan.

6. Bake in the oven at 325 degrees for about 40 minutes.

7. Cool in the pan overnight.

8. Cut into squares.

Chapter 7

When we get to class the next morning, Ms. Tomasso has her word of the day on the board. Today's word is HEROES.

"Okay, good morning, everyone. Get writing." She rarely smiles when she talks, and it makes me think she's mad. All the time. I know she isn't angry, and I know people don't have to smile all the time, but still. It starts the day off on a tense note, and I don't like it.

"I know what you're gonna write about," Ava whispers to me. She digs through the desk to find a pen and her writing journal.

"You do?" I whisper back.

"Duh, your grandparents." She smiles.

"Oh, yeah." I smile. "My mind didn't go in that direction for some reason, but good idea. Thank you!"

To be honest, I hadn't really thought of them, and my mind was kind of blank thinking I didn't have a hero. I don't want to admit that though—not to Ava, not even to myself. I guess I didn't think of them as heroes because they're just regular, run-of-the-mill people who show up and do their jobs and care about us and all of that. But truthfully, all of that is pretty heroic.

"Who are you gonna write about?" I whisper to Ava.

"Girls!" Ms. Tomasso screeches from her desk. "This is independent, quiet writing time. We're almost in October. You should know this."

October.

Halloween is soon. Very, very soon. How is it possible that Ava and I haven't discussed costumes yet? Same with Sally, Aanya, and Brynn. They're usually obsessed with Halloween.

"Ellie," Ms. Tomasso calls out, and I swear she always has eyes on me. "I don't see your pencil moving."

I nod and smile. I'm about to tell her that I've been *thinking* this whole time, but I don't want to distract anyone, so instead I take out my pen and start scribbling.

Hero. What a funny word since it also means a sandwich. I guess that makes sense for me though, especially since my heroes are my grandparents, and they own a deli. Haha, it sounds funny but I'm being completely serious.

Lukshen Deli has been in my family for four generations. My great-grandmother started it, and it's still here feeding the people of Marlborough Lake like it has been doing for decades.

But my grandparents aren't my heroes because they own a deli, though that is very cool. They are my heroes because they work hard, and they don't quit when things get tough.

"Pencils down, students," Ms. Tomasso says, and it's annoying because I was finally getting into this assignment.

She doesn't ever really give us enough time to finish and then the next day we just get a new word. I wonder what the point of that is. If I were feeling more confident in myself, I'd ask her.

At lunch, I decide that I need to bring up Halloween. It always takes us forever to figure out costumes and I can't wait any longer.

"Guys, can you believe it's almost October?" I ask them.

"I cannot," Sally says. "We're getting to the part of the year where my gram comes to live with us, and I hate it."

"Doesn't she live in Florida? Why does she come here for the winter? It's confusing," Brynn says and takes a giant bite of her apple.

"She likes to be here for Christmas and my parents like to be home for Christmas, so she lives with us from November to January. It's a very special kind of torture," says Sally.

We all crack up because Sally is probably the funniest person in our school, maybe even our town. Sometimes I don't know if she's trying to be funny or if everything she says just comes out that way. Her dad is a writer for comedy TV shows, though, so maybe it's genetic.

"Why do you hate your grandma so much?" Nina asks, and the whole table kind of gasps. Nina just comes out and asks stuff, all blunt and alarming, like she's starting little fires in the middle of the lunch table.

"I don't hate her. I guess it's just that she thinks she's in charge of me," Sally explains. "Of course I don't *hate her* hate her. She gives the best hugs."

"Bubbie could probably challenge her in a hugging competition," I say, laughing.

"Well, I love your family, Sally," Ava cuts in.

"I do, too. Obviously. Of course I love them." Sally shrugs.

Nina's face turns bright red, and she stares down at her empty reusable bowl of pasta.

"Are you okay?" Ava asks her.

Nina exhales. "Yeah, my grandma died before I was born and sometimes I wonder what it would be like if she was around. I think my life would be sooo different."

We're all silent then. I don't know the right answer or reply, and I actually don't even know if there is a right answer or reply.

"I get that," Sally replies. "Like how one thing drastically changes everything. We're talking about my dad's mom. But my mom's mom, my meemaw, died when she was little and she wonders about that kind of stuff all the time."

Nina nods, still seeming unable to speak, like maybe she's never talked about this before.

Ava puts a hand on Nina's shoulder and then takes it away fast.

"That's why pictures and videos and stuff are so important." Ava pauses. "Am I the only one who is obsessed with looking at pictures of my mom from when she was a kid? She was super cute!"

Ava looks around the table and so do I. Everyone starts nodding.

"I love it, too," Brynn says.

"Same," Aanya adds.

All of a sudden, an amazing, over-the-top awesome feeling comes over me, like everything is somehow the way it's meant to be. Our group of friends is totally connecting on something real, something deep, something maybe not everyone talks about. Family and life and memories. I'm proud of that. I'm so happy to be a part of it. I hope to share this kind of feeling with my own kids one day, when I'm way older. Bubbie says it's called *l'dor v'dor*, a connection from generation to generation. Maybe one day future generations will be looking at pictures of me right now.

Pride is a good thing.

Pride can take me really far, I bet.

I need to remember that more often.

Chapter 8

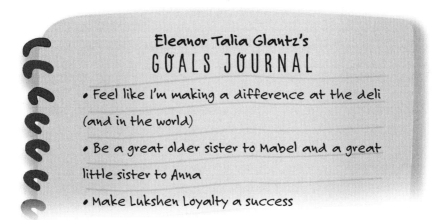

Eleanor Talia Glantz's
GOALS JOURNAL
- Feel like I'm making a difference at the deli (and in the world)
- Be a great older sister to Mabel and a great little sister to Anna
- Make Lukshen Loyalty a success

When Ava and I get to my house after school, Anna and a few of her friends are sitting around the kitchen table. They're deep in conversation, like they're solving all of the world's problems right now.

They talk with their hands and yell and get fired up. I wonder what they're talking about.

"Do you think we'll be like that when we're in high school?" Ava asks me on the way up the stairs. We're each carrying a can of seltzer and a bag of mini pretzels.

"Maybe?" I shrug. "Anna has always been so intense, though. Do you think I'm intense?"

Ava considers this for a second. "Um, kinda sorta sometimes." She giggles. "Not all the time. Definitely not as intense as Anna is. And I'd say Mabel is the least intense."

"Yeah, for sure. But she's basically a baby, so . . ."

"Right." Ava smiles.

We sit on my bungee chairs, eat our snacks, and talk about the idea for the Lukshen Loyalty program.

"I feel so good that this is our first step," I tell Ava, crunching a pretzel. "People enjoy feeling like they're a part of stuff, ya know?"

"Definitely, yeah."

I look at our empty bags of pretzels. "We need more snacks. Let's go find some."

Ava shrugs and follows me down the stairs, where we find our mailman, Jerry, sitting at the kitchen table with Mom.

"Hey, Jerry," I say.

"Oh, hi, girls!"

I wonder if most kids our age are this friendly with their mail carrier. I'm thinking probably not, but I guess I don't know for sure. Jerry and my mom grew up together, though. They were in the same class every single grade of elementary school. So, he's not only our mail carrier—he's our family friend.

Ava and I go to the pantry for another snack and then we hang back a little to eavesdrop on this conversation. It's not every day that Jerry's at our kitchen table—he's kind of like a local celebrity—and to be honest, I'm a little curious about what's happening.

"I can't do the walking anymore," Jerry says. "I feel worn out. I thought the meds would help, but so far, not really." He pauses. "I wanted to let you know that next week will be my last week. And I'll miss seeing you."

Ava and I look at each other, wide-eyed. Jerry no longer our mail carrier?! How could this be?

"I can't believe I'm retiring at forty-eight. I don't want to retire, but such is life. Such is life."

This gives me an idea. I grab Ava's hand and pull her up the stairs. We make it to my room with more snacks, and I quickly the door.

"Jerry!" I shriek.

"I know." She sits down on my window seat and opens a bag of dried fruit. "It's so sad."

"You're not thinking what I'm thinking?" I ask her.

"Um." She laughs. "Not sure what you're thinking here, El. I can usually read your brain, but this time it's a little unclear."

"Jerry will be the new Lukshen Deli delivery person!" I yell, and then cover my mouth, a little worried he'll hear. "He doesn't want to retire! He can't walk long distances but that doesn't mean he can't *drive* to deliver orders! So many people already know him, and they'll be happy seeing him deliver their food."

She's quiet, thinking about it.

"Don't you think it's a genius idea?" I ask. "And we can get the deliveries up and running soon, so it's all in place when winter starts and no one wants to go outside."

"I do think it's pretty smart, El. But we don't even know if Jerry would want to do it."

"So?" I pace back and forth in my room, nibbling at my pinky nail. "After we hear him leave, we'll run down and ask my mom what she thinks, and then maybe we can talk to him about it! But look at it this way, it'll help the deli and help Jerry and it'll all be ah-may-zing!" I sing the last word, vibrating with enthusiasm for this idea and feeling proud I thought of it.

I look out my window; Anna and her friends are still screaming, but now they're on the back deck. I'm kind of surprised Mom hasn't gone out there yet and asked them to stop.

"Anna and her friends drive, too," Ava reminds me. "They could also be delivery people." She claps and then starts writing things down on the notepad I always keep on my desk. "We're changing things up. A delivery thing up and running, Lukshen Loyalty."

"Okay." I just hope we're making progress fast enough.

I just want to get to the end where everything feels okay, and the deli is safe and we're all safe and I don't have anything else to worry about.

I wonder if anyone ever gets to a place in time where they don't have anything else to worry about.

"Let's go outside and see what's up with Anna and her friends," I say, feeling like I need a distraction from the worrying.

Ava shrugs. "Okay."

When we get out to the backyard, they all stop their yelling and look at us, so I just say hi. Then Ava and I walk over to the hammock and start swaying back and forth together.

Now that we're out here, they stop talking and I have no idea what all the yelling was about. I'll admit—I'm kind of disappointed because I was really curious to know.

We could go back in and see if Jerry has left and talk to my mom about that, but I'm comfy on the hammock now and I don't want to get up.

"Why are you guys out here?" Anna stands over us. "We're in the middle of something. You have the whole house. Mabel isn't even home."

She's quiet for a moment and I think she's going to explode and scream in our faces. Instead, she gets closer to us and says, "Listen, Cybil is going through a really bad time. She just found out her dad has all this credit card debt they didn't know about and she's trying to find a way to help them. Okay? Please go back inside so we can help her."

Ava and I make eyes at each other.

For once I really do know what Ava's thinking, but I also know it isn't the time to suggest Cybil become a Lukshen Deli delivery person.

I'll save that for later.

Also, I wonder, how many delivery people do we need? I guess it depends on how many people will order delivery. And I guess that depends on how they'll even access the menu or place the orders. I don't know if it would be over the phone or on a website or what.

"You're still just sitting here, Ellie. Please go inside."

Anna looks like she's about to cry, so Ava and I get up and change locations for what feels like the millionth time.

We go into the den and turn on a cartoon just so no one overhears our conversation.

"I think Lukshen needs a website," I tell Ava. "Like right now. That'll be the thing that ties it all together—loyalty programs and delivery orders and all the stuff."

"I have to admit it's always seemed kind of silly to me that you don't have a website," Ava laughs a little.

"Stop. Don't laugh at us. We're old-fashioned. We've been around for over a hundred years!"

"I know. And I love you." She scootches closer to me on the couch. "You know, my dad's a web designer. Duh. Of course you know. This is the easiest thing to solve and look how long it took us to get there!"

"Duh! Your dad!" I lean my head back. "It seems like sometimes the most obvious things are hidden. Do you know what I mean?"

"I do. I really, really do."

KASHA PENYA

INGREDIENTS
1 cup brown rice
3 cups baby lima beans
1 tablespoon canola oil
Salt and pepper to taste
6 or more large onions, diced

INSTRUCTIONS
1. Wash the rice thoroughly. Cook until soft. Drain.

2. Soak the lima beans overnight. Cook until mushy. Do not drain—the water should absorb. Cover the pot while cooking!

3. Saute the onions in oil.

4. Combine all these parts. Season to taste. It can be baked in a 350 degree oven up to 30 minutes if you prefer it dry over liquid.

Chapter 9

After Ava leaves, I try to get a good night's sleep, but Mabel spends the entire night coughing, so I spend the entire night awake, staring at my ceiling and praying to fall asleep.

I'm a zombie the next morning when I come down the stairs and hear Anna at the kitchen table crying to my parents.

"I'm sorry Cybil is going through this," Dad says while buttering a piece of raisin toast, his ultimate favorite breakfast.

"What are they going to do? How can we help them? We can't just stand by and not do anything." Anna holds her phone at the table. Her plate of eggs is untouched, starting to get goopy and weird-looking.

"El, you want cheesy eggs?" Mom asks from the stove. I nod. I pour myself a glass of orange juice and sit down at the table.

"I can't believe you guys don't have any ideas," Anna says, looking back and forth from Dad to Mom and then from Mom to Dad.

"Anna," Mom says, bringing me my plate of cheesy eggs. "There's only so much we can do for them. We can support them, be there for them, bring meals, and have them over for dinner and talk things through. All of that. Can we solve all their problems? No. I wish we could."

"I have an idea, actually," I say after a bite of eggs. I wipe a little speck of cheese from the corner of my mouth.

I expect Anna to tell me to be quiet and not get involved, but she doesn't. She smiles, and maybe she actually wants to hear what I have to say. Somehow she's softened since our trip to the stationery store.

"Tell us," Anna says to me.

My parents eye each other, like they're a little curious, too.

"Cybil can be a Lukshen Deli delivery person!" I exclaim. Then I sip my orange juice, all casual, waiting to see their reaction.

"Ellie, we don't do delivery," Anna says, matter-of-fact, like I'm a child who needs to be spoken to in very simple words. So, I guess she hasn't softened completely.

"That's an interesting idea, El," Mom says. Dad nods.

We're all quiet after that and I want to continue making my point, but I also think it'll be more effective if I just kind of let it sit there in the air for a little bit.

Plus, I'm going to the deli after school today, and I plan to talk to Bubbie about it. She's always the person in the family most open to my ideas anyway.

It's one of the zillion reasons why I think she's the best human on Earth.

The phone rings a minute later, and I answer. I'm the only person I know who has a landline, but my mom thinks it's "cozy." The only people who call it, though, are Bubbie, Zeyda, and sometimes telemarketers.

This time, it's Zeyda.

"Ellie!" Zeyda says after I say hello. "How are you?"

I don't know how it's possible for Zeyda to always maintain this level of enthusiasm. It's like he's always excited. Literally. Always. Even if he's watching a boring show or sports game or driving in traffic. He seems to always find some element of every part of life exciting.

"I'm good. Getting ready for school," I say, trying to match his energy level, but I can't seem to do it. It's still morning, after all.

"Wonderful. Have a fantastic day! Please put Mom on."

I hand Mom the phone and go to finish my eggs but try hard to eavesdrop on the conversation, just in case I can get any clues about the deli.

"I see," Mom says. Pause. "Right." Pause. "There's a lot to consider." Pause. "Mm. Hmm." Pause. "Okay, Dad, love ya, we'll discuss in a bit when I get over there, run the numbers and everything." Then she hangs up.

Run the numbers?

That has to be about the deli.

I make eyes at Anna, who is not paying attention at all. She's texting furiously as if she's going to solve all the world's problems right this minute just by using her phone.

Mabel is still coughing upstairs.

"Okay, so you're home with Mabes today?" Mom says to Dad. "I'm heading to the deli. Will fill you in later."

Dad looks up from the paper. He's probably the last remaining human to read a paper newspaper, but I love that about him. I guess it kind of goes with the cozy vibe, the way Mom feels about the landline. "Yes and yes. Love you."

"Love you," Mom replies in a worn-out sort of way.

"So, what did Zeyda call about?" I ask, trying to sound totally chill, like I don't care that much when the truth is I actually care more than anything.

"Nothing really." Mom sighs. "I gotta run. Love you all."

Anna, Dad, and I stay at the table for a few more moments. Then I meet Ava outside for our walk to the bus.

"Okay, so listen to this," Ava says as soon as she sees me.

"Listening . . ."

"Nina texted me and she's having a major, major, major twelfth birthday party," she starts. "Like, epic. Everyone in the grade. She's getting a DJ and stuff, too."

"Okay." I swallow back the immediate sting that Nina didn't text me about it.

"So, I figured you'd be excited. You love parties." She stops walking and pulls her hood up onto her head. "And everyone is invited!"

"Yeah! So happy to hear that." I pause to think for a second. "Also, kind of wild that she's turning twelve in November of sixth grade. She's a full year older than I am!"

"Cutoff dates were different in her old school," Ava explains. "I mean, there's a bunch of kids who are way older than you because they have late birthdays and repeated pre-k! You're just the baby of the grade."

"Ah. Okay. Right." I make a frowny face and put an arm over her shoulder. "Oh well. My mom says I'll appreciate it when I'm older!"

When we get to our lockers, everyone is yapping about Nina's party, like they already knew about it.

"We're definitely having a DJ, and there will be a photo booth, and also *so much* swag," Nina explains, flipping her head over and then pulling her hair into a tight ballerina bun. "Epic giveaways, too."

While everyone is going on and on about the party, I sort of stay quiet, only chiming in every few minutes. I'm feeling left out but my mind isn't here, anyway. It's totally back at home, in the kitchen, thinking about that Zeyda call.

My family is definitely making decisions about the deli without me, and they may be irreversible decisions. They don't know about my plans yet for delivery and Lukshen Loyalty. They don't know how I have all these ideas about how to revive the deli.

My heart starts pounding and my skin gets all clammy. I suddenly feel like I have the energy to run three marathons, but also like I'm about to pass out in the hallway at the same time.

I need to get out of here.

I need to get to the deli before they do something drastic that can't be changed.

I may only be eleven, but they need to know my ideas and how they can work and how Lukshen Deli can be a true success again.

"Ellie?" Ava asks, looking at me with curvy eyebrows. "You okay?"

"I don't feel well," I admit. "I need to go."

"Want me to take you to the nurse?" Ava asks.

"I'm okay, thank you, though."

I grab my backpack, hoist it up over my shoulders, and head down the hall to the nurse. I don't even bother saying goodbye to the others because I really don't want to get into a whole discussion about everything. Plus, they're so consumed by talking about Nina's party, they probably wouldn't notice me anyway.

All I know is I need to get out of here, and I need to get out of here fast.

I can't let this whole thing slip away because I waited too long to speak up.

When I get to Nurse Wilkinson's office, she's taking a kid's temperature and I feel antsy that she's not able to talk to me right away.

I can't lose a single second here. Mom could be at the deli with Bubbie and Zeyda right now, signing some papers and selling the deli away right this minute.

"Hi, um, sorry to interrupt." I pause. "I don't feel great, but I live super close to school, so can I just go home?" I ask, as sweetly as possible.

"Sweetie, no." Nurse Wilkinson smiles. "I'll need to call someone at home. Okay? Just take a seat over there and I'll be with you as soon as I can."

I nod and try not to appear flustered. I expected this. It was worth a shot, though.

I sit down on a wobbly folding chair and listen to the loud ticking of the clock above the desk. It feels like a million years pass before Nurse Wilkinson comes to talk to me.

"So, tell me what's wrong," she says in her soft, soothing tone.

"I just need to go home. I don't feel quite right."

"Can you explain your symptoms?" she asks, reaching over to grab the forehead-scanning thermometer.

"I have a weird stomach feeling. Please, can you just call my house so someone can pick me up?" I look away so I don't meet her gaze. I feel bad lying to the nurse.

"Anything else going on, sweetie?" She looks at me sideways, perplexed. "Stuff going on at home?"

I hesitate to answer. I usually hate the word "sweetie," but when Nurse Wilkinson says it, it sounds genuine. "I just don't feel right. I can't focus. I have a lot on my mind."

She nods. "Sort of like spiraling thoughts?"

I bite my bottom lip. Somehow, it's like she knows what I'm going through. "Yeah, exactly."

"We all have days like that," she says. "It's good you can recognize it."

She sits with me for another moment, and we talk about feelings and stress and how to calm ourselves down.

"Deep calming breaths always help at least a little bit." Nurse Wilkinson smiles. "Try it when nothing else seems to help."

I nod, and we sit quietly together for another moment or two. Then she finds my parents' number in the school directory and calls home.

"Hello? Hi. I have Ellie here in the nurse's office. She says she's not feeling well." Pause. "Mm-hmm. Yeah. I think it would be best for her to take the day and rest at home." Pause. "Mm-hmm. Okay. Thank you."

I look at her, wide-eyed and nervous, hopeful the answer is that someone is coming to get me right away.

"Your mom should be here in ten minutes or so," the nurse says. "Put your head back and close your eyes and try to relax in the meantime, okay? And remember: deep breaths."

I try to sit there patiently in the chair, propping my coat behind my head and leaning back against the wall. I try not to think about how much time is passing.

But the longer it takes, the more I feel like my parents aren't concerned at all that I'm not feeling well, which is super strange considering Mabel is home sick, so they should be worried I'm sick, too.

Also, the longer it takes, the more worried I am that they're signing the deli away right this minute, giving up on it, or deciding that we need to move, that we can't afford to live here.

I need to get there. I need to stop them.

Chapter 10

Eleanor Talia Glantz's
GOALS JOURNAL

- Become better friends with Nina
- Convince my parents that we have a lot of things to try to boost business at the deli
- Become more of a morning person

After I've been freezing and sweating at the same time for what feels like three hundred years, Mom finally shows up.

"Hi, Ellie. Come on, let's get you home," she says.

"Feel better, Ellie," Nurse Wilkinson says as I pick up my backpack. "We just got some of these pamphlets in the mail; one might be helpful reading for you." She smiles her soft smile again, and I put the pamphlet in my backpack.

Mom and I walk down the hall together. When we get to the car, I sit in the front seat mostly so I can put on the butt warmer. It's so soothing. We have an older car, so we don't have them in the back seats. Thank goodness I'm finally old enough to sit in the front now!

"You okay, El?" Mom asks, sounding concerned but also distracted.

"Yeah," I say. "Just weird stomach stuff." I pause, feeling the urge to speak up about what's really on my mind.

"Mom, what's going on with the deli? You can talk to me, you know. Please don't treat me like I'm a little kid. I'm not Mabel. I'm also not Anna. I actually care, and I'm old enough to know the real stuff." I pause to catch my breath.

"Ellie. You don't need to worry about this. It doesn't concern you."

"But that's not true!"

Mom sighs. "I just want you to focus on kid stuff." She pauses. "Don't feel consumed by adult matters."

After that, we're quiet the rest of the ride home. I'm starting to think she's onto me; she must know I'm not sick with stomach stuff, that there's more going on.

As soon as we walk into the house, Mabel pulls me in close for a whisper.

"Last night before bed, I did this thing where I swallowed half the bottle of those hot red pepper flakes Dad puts on pizza, so I'd cough and then act all weak, and they let me stay home," she whispers directly in my ear, so fiercely that I feel some of her spit on my earlobe. Gross.

"Why are you faking sick to stay home, Mabes? You're in second grade. And school just started," I remind her. "Also, you really coughed a *lot* last night for someone who was faking."

She shrugs. "Needed a mental health day."

I burst out laughing. I have no idea where she gets this stuff. But I guess she's onto something. I clearly need a mental health day, too.

Mabel plops herself down on the couch and turns on some random cartoon. I decide to sit and watch it with her and give Mom a moment or two to cool off before I start interrogating her again.

We're interrupted when Dad comes in, though, walks right up to the TV, and turns it off. He sits down on the edge of the ottoman like he doesn't have time to relax all the way back in the chair.

Then he leans forward, elbows on his knees.

"Okay, girls." He starts and then stops. "A couple things. First of all, I know everyone needs a day to recharge every now and then, so let's just put that out in the open, and if that's what you need, please say so." He pauses. "Okay?"

We look at each other, eye bulge, and then nod, half smiling at Dad.

"Second of all, there's a lot going on right now. Mom is a firm believer in not stressing out or oversharing with you guys, and I am a firm believer in that, too, but I also believe in honesty, so we're at a bit of a crossroads there."

Sometimes Dad talks so much, I have to zone out in the middle, then I try to pick back up where I left off and then I lose track of what he's saying. But it's almost impossible to pay attention to him the entire time he's speaking.

"Um, Dad. Please get to the point," Mabel says.

Thankfully I have little Mabes, who always says what's on her mind. She kind of speaks my thoughts in a way, and I'm grateful for that.

"Bubbie hasn't been feeling well; she's been having on-and-off health issues for a while that seem to be getting worse lately," Dad says. "It's nothing we're overly worried about yet, but you should know Mom is very overwhelmed with this and with the deli and managing everything, so I just want to focus on us being patient with her, and trying to be our very best selves."

My heart pounds with worry about Bubbie. I repeat the "it's nothing we're overly worried about yet" over and over in my head.

If they're not worried, I don't need to worry. That's what I tell myself.

"First of all, you know I'm gonna worry about Bubbie, Dad, no matter what you say." I twist some hair around my finger. "So . . . let's just put that out there."

"Ellie." He sighs. "Let's try to keep the worry to a minimum at least. Worry doesn't really accomplish anything."

Obviously, I know that, but it still doesn't help me not worry. Why doesn't he understand? I need to change the topic.

"Fine, whatever you say. But also, I need to speak up about something before it's too late. I have a lot of ideas to save the deli and really ramp up business and I'm already working on them, so please listen to me."

Mabel cracks up. "I don't think you're in charge of this. But okay."

"I'm serious," I continue. "I know it's been slow lately, but there are things we can do to help."

Dad sighs. "Yes. Maybe. Possibly. I don't know."

Mabel and I make eyes at each other and try not to laugh. Somehow, Dad manages to use so many words even when he's trying to say he doesn't know or doesn't have an answer.

"Well, try to relax today, you two, because tomorrow you'll be back at school," Dad says. "Mom is going with Bubbie to the doctor. I'm trying to get some deli paperwork done upstairs."

He leaves the room and I feel frozen on this couch.

"Think we can order in pizza?" Mabel asks me.

I shrug. "I don't think I can eat. My stomach is on its own roller coaster right now."

"Hm." Mabel twists her legs around, so her feet are now underneath the blanket. "I can always eat."

Oh, to be Mabel Glantz. The blissful life of a seven-year-old. I hope I appreciated it when I was that age. I think I did, but I was always a worrier. Lucky for Mabel, she doesn't seem to be that way.

Mabel and I spend the next three hours watching TV. I'm so bored because she only wants to watch little kid shows, and after a while, I start to wish I was at school. Plus, I have a sinking sort of feeling settling in my throat that drifts down to my stomach. I'm not at lunch. Nina's probably going on and on about her party, and I'm not there. So, when I'm back tomorrow, I'll immediately feel left out and sort of need to backtrack and figure out what I missed.

I start to count the hours until school's over and Ava gets home. Right now, I feel like I'm floating between two worlds, school world and home world, and this in-between just doesn't seem right.

All I want right now is to get to the deli, so I can get to the soup and make some more wishes. Sometimes the soup needs extra time to work—especially for big wishes like these.

The most important one is for Bubbie to be okay.

I need her to be okay.

MOCK KISHKE

INGREDIENTS

2 or 3 celery stalks
2 or 3 carrots
1 onion
12 ounces crackers
¼ pound butter
2 teaspoons of sugar

INSTRUCTIONS

1. Grind all the ingredients together.

2. Roll into kishke shapes, like long sausages.

3. Wrap in regular foil.

4. Bake for 35 to 40 minutes at 350 degrees.

Chapter 11

At three o'clock, the phone rings, and I expect it to be one of my teachers checking in or maybe just calling to remind my parents that I still need to complete the homework. I'm wrong though—it's Bubbie.

"Hi, Ellie-doll," she says.

"Hi!" I say, overwhelmed with relief. Bubbie can't be that sick if she's calling me right now. Her voice sounds strong and normal and fine.

This is amazing. This may be the best call I've ever gotten.

"I'm coming to pick you up. I need help at the deli, and I can't stand the thought of your eyes looking at the TV for hours on end." She pauses. "Get your coat on and meet me outside."

"Mabel, too?" I ask, My heart is pounding that Bubbie feels well enough to drive.

"Just you," she says. Clearly she knows I'm not physically sick.

"But Mabel wasn't really si—"

She doesn't let me finish. "Just you, Ellie-doll. Meet me outside."

Bubbie sits in the car in the driveway waiting patiently for me to come out. She listens to a podcast, staring out the window, and even if takes me forever to get outside, she doesn't say things like "it took you long enough" or anything like that.

She just waits.

"Hi, doll," she says, in her cheery tone as soon as I get into the car. I try to read her voice and her expressions to figure out if she's worried about her health, or if she's worried about the deli and how we'll have money and if we'll all need to move.

Nothing.

Bubbie is her usual bubbly self. Maybe Dad was overreacting; maybe she's not that sick. Maybe it's just a super small thing.

We drive to the deli and she's listening to some podcast about the need for rest in difficult times. I zone in and out, but the voice is very soothing.

"So happy to have you with me, Ellie-doll." Bubbie glances over at me from her seat, grabs my hand, and holds it for a moment, driving with one hand on the steering wheel. I look at our hands together and feel little pains in my heart. I want

to freeze this moment. I want to always remember what our hands look like together.

A few minutes later, we get to the deli and hop out of the car. Lukshen Deli smells are the best smells in the world, and they surround me like a cloud as I walk inside: brisket marinating in the oven, all sweet and salty at the same time, and the most soothing chicken soup in the pot, like the smell alone could heal me. Plus, there's the oily-but-not-greasy smell of crinkle-cut fries at just the perfect level of crispness in the fryer.

These smells mix together, and I breathe them all in, wanting to memorize them, having this overwhelming feeling that they may not be mine forever. That one day they'll be gone. That maybe I took the whole concept of Ellie's Deli for granted.

Bubbie immediately checks in with the people working today—Stacy at the cash register and Barry, our accountant, who's here today to go over some paperwork.

I walk over to the soup and stare deep into the pot. I focus on the little bubbles and breathe in the salty magic.

Please let Bubbie not be sick. Please let it be a mistake. Please let her stay healthy. Please let business at the deli really pick up and let everything be fine. Thank you, masterful brothy powers. Thank you so much.

Okay, that was a lot of wishes, I know that. But sometimes I just need to do that. It becomes more like praying than wishing and I know that's weird, but it's comforting to me. It's sort of like my own version of the Mi Shebeirach, the actual prayer for healing.

I believe in the power of soup: healing properties for sick people, comforting properties for those that are suffering emotional stuff, and magical powers for me. Magical powers to make my wishes heard and make them come true.

Customers trickle in over the course of the afternoon and evening. Some teenagers stroll through and get a giant knish and a few bottles of soda; some old ladies buy soup to stock up their freezers; and some frenzied moms come for our fried chicken family dinner special.

"This special has saved my life so many times," one mom says to Bubbie, brushing the sticky strands of hair away from her forehead. She has two kids in a stroller with her. "I don't understand how people expect moms to do it all: shuttle kids to activities, cook, clean the house, look presentable. It's impossible!"

"Darling, you're amazing. You're doing a fabulous job. Please. Give yourself a break sometime, okay?" Bubbie smiles her soft smile as she finishes packing up the food.

The mom looks a little choked up. "I needed to hear that. I really did."

"It's the truth. Come in every day, and I'll say the same thing. You're doing great."

Stacy tallies up the order and swipes the credit card, and soon this mom with the double stroller is on her way out. I look over at Bubbie but she doesn't make eye contact with me.

This mom is definitely coming in here for more than the fried chicken family special. There's more going on here than food. I always knew that; I definitely did. But now I realize it on a different level.

These people need Bubbie. And she needs them.

Nothing can happen to Bubbie, not now, not ever. I want to cover her in bubble wrap or something, give her every vitamin possible. I'm not a doctor, but I have this belief that the right vitamins and medicines can help people live a very long time.

I spend the rest of the afternoon observing Bubbie with the customers and wondering if Ava is going to text me.

She doesn't, and my mind flip-flops between worrying about my friends, worrying if Bubbie is really sick, and worrying about the deli.

"Stace, you can go," Bubbie calls out to her around five. "I'll take care of everything from here on out. Go home to your beautiful baby."

"Are you sure?" Stacy asks.

"More than sure." Bubbie smiles.

Soon it's just the two of us at the deli and Bubbie goes to the office to organize the supplies. I'm at the front, noshing on some half sour pickles and flipping through all the restaurant supplier catalogues Bubbie gets, when a little old man comes traipsing in.

"Is Harriet here?" he asks.

Harriet is Bubbie's real name.

"She's in the back, I think." I smile. "I'll go get her."

He's the cutest little man I've ever seen. Probably about my height, wearing a wool cap and a windbreaker jacket. He looks familiar but I don't know his name.

"Bub." I knock on the door. "Someone's here for you."

She leaves the office and calls out, "Norman! How have you been? I was planning to check in on you tomorrow. I wanted to give you a day of peace; I'm sure everyone in Marlborough Lake is calling you a hundred times a day."

"A hundred and one," he says as Bubbie walks over to him.

They sit down at a table together and Norman says, "I'm okay. But listen, Harri, I have a favor to ask you. It's a little unconventional, so just a warning . . ."

Now I'm intrigued. This little old man seems to know my Bubbie so well.

Bubbie laughs her throaty laugh. "You must have enough food for an army! But anything for you, Normie."

Normie?

"I missed the minyan at my synagogue this morning. I'm embarrassed to say it, but I slept through it. I want to say Kaddish for Rena, but I don't want to say it alone. And I know we're not even ten people, but this is the only place I could think to go. The other synagogues are too far." He shrugs. "See what I mean? Unconventional."

The Kaddish is a memorial prayer that Jews say when they've lost a loved one. Typically, you say it with a minyan, or ten people who have had their bar or bat mitzvah already. A bar or bat mitzvah is an important celebration in Judaism to celebrate a person's coming of age.

"It's perfectly fine with me. I'm honored you thought of me, and thought of Lukshen," says Bubbie.

He smiles. "You're the best."

"I can say it, too!" I say, walking over to them, making it clear I was eavesdropping. "I mean, I haven't had my bat mitzvah yet, but I can stand with you. It's the thought that counts, right?"

"That's so lovely, Ellie," Norman says.

"Isn't she a gem?" Bubbie beams.

Bubbie and Norman say the Kaddish and I join in, feeling proud that I know this prayer and confident in my Hebrew.

They hug when they finish, and Bubbie gives him three containers of matzo ball soup, no charge, and a bag of sour pickles. His favorite, apparently.

After Norman leaves, we close up and drive home. We're almost at my house when another brilliant idea floods my brain.

"Bub!"

"What? Oh, Ellie! Don't yell in the car. You startled me!"

"Sorry, sorry." I deflate a little. "But I just had an idea! We should have a nightly minyan at Lukshen! Norman said that the synagogue only has it in the morning, and clearly he slept through it, so I bet a lot of people sleep through it. We could be fulfilling a real need! You obviously know the prayer. People could come in and say it, and get dinner, and it could be so comforting to everyone. A real community! And I bet we could get ten people every night once we get started with it!"

"Oh, Ellie. This was just one time. I'm not sure people want to say Kaddish in a deli." She turns to me. "But you're a delightful, clever girl for even thinking about it! So wise beyond your years. So beautiful!" She shakes her head. "Oy, you're so delicious, I want to eat you up."

"Okay, Bub." I widen my eyes. "Chill. Please chill."

"I am chill." She laughs. "But you're the best."

Bubbie parks in the driveway and comes inside. My parents and Zeyda are sitting in the den with Anna and Mabel watching some competition singing show. It seems like there are so many of these shows I can barely keep them straight anymore.

I go upstairs to start homework, and that's when I realize I don't actually know what the homework is since I wasn't in school today. And that's when I realize Ava *still* hasn't checked in, not even once!

"Ava!" I say into the screen as soon as she answers my video call.

"Oh, hey, El." She's clearly watching TV as she talks to me.

"Um, what's going on? You don't even call to check in on your sick friend?" I blurt out, not being able to hold in my rage.

"Ellie." She stares directly at me through the screen. "We both know you weren't sick."

"You knew I wasn't sick?"

"Ellie, you've been my best friend and next-door neighbor since birth. I know everything you know about yourself and more," she says.

"Fine. Actually, maybe I wasn't physically sick, but I was feeling super anxious, and that counts too," I explain.

"That's true. Are you feeling better?" Ava asks.

I shrug. "Kinda. Sorta." I pause. "Anyway. How was the rest of the day?"

"Nothing special," she answers. "Nina told us more about her party. Her mom's best friend is a party planner, like for celebrities and stuff, so that's why it's so over the top. Don't be too jealous."

"Okay. I wasn't jealous."

"Yeah, you were. Again, I know everything you know about yourself and more." Ava laughs at herself. "Okay, I gotta go.

There's no nightly homework, just the stuff we have for the week. See you in the morning for the bus?"

"Yup. See you then."

We hang up the call and I'm left feeling kind of worn out. I'm not sure how this day felt so long and complicated. I get in my pajamas and go to the bathroom to brush my teeth, but I stop when I'm halfway there, overhearing my parents talk in their bedroom; their door is open a crack.

"We can't tell them during the week," Dad says. "They're busy and preoccupied with school. Our seven-year-old already wanted a mental health day!" He laughs. "Let's wait until next Friday. Give it another week."

"I hate having this hang over my head, Ben," Mom says. "I really do. I need to finalize this, tell the girls, and move forward."

"I know, I know."

I hear their bedroom door close, and Mabel yell out a goodnight that no one responds to. I wonder if Mabel heard them, too, and what she thinks. Or if she's oblivious to all of this.

I know I won't be sleeping much tonight, my worry creeping up again. Maybe I'll take out that pamphlet Nurse Wilkinson gave me about anxiety and calming down worrisome thoughts.

I hope it helps.

Chapter 12

Eleanor Talia Glantz's
GOALS JOURNAL
- Be open and honest with my friends
- Try to be a more "one day at a time" person
- Eat more vegetables

The next day at school, after math class, Ava and I go to our lockers to put stuff away before lunch. She's acting strange—all aloof and far-away feeling.

"Ava. I need to talk to you," I say, after closing my locker door. "Tell me what's going on this instant."

"Um." She closes her locker door and stands in front of me, hands on her hips. "Why? No clue what's going on right now."

"Yes, you do. You've overheard more stuff about the deli. Something new. I can tell." I open my eyes wide and try to keep my tone light, even though my insides are twisty. "I've known you since preschool and I can read your mind!"

"Ellie! Okay. I don't know much for real, which is why I haven't said anything. You know my favorite hobby is eavesdropping, but that doesn't mean *everything* I hear is true."

"Well, I love eavesdropping too, so between what I hear and what you hear, things may make sense. It's all part of a puzzle. Things are shifting all around me and it feels eerie and bad." I pause. "I don't like it. You need to help me."

Ava's eyes soften. "All I heard is that a restaurant group wants to come in and revitalize Marlborough Lake's restaurant row since they're putting in that new concert hall thing. So, basically, the restaurant group wants to buy Lukshen. They want to keep it a deli, but more like a theme restaurant kind of deli. It won't be kosher, I don't think. They want to revamp Taste of India, too—ya know, the place that Aanya's cousin owns—and put in a fancy juice bar down the street, make the Chinese restaurant more Asian fusion-like, adding sushi and some Thai dishes, too . . ."

"I knew you knew stuff!" I say. "You overheard all of this! You know a lot!"

She leans against the locker. "You know I'm a good eavesdropper."

"I don't think there's anything we can do, then, if the restaurant group wants to pay a lot of money to take over . . ." I slump down against the locker and fall to the floor. "And we need money, or we'll have to sell the house and move . . . it's like, either way I lose something."

Ava sits beside me and puts her arm over my shoulders. "Maybe let your parents worry about this, El. I know we love brainstorming ideas for the deli, and it's fun and stuff, but you're only eleven. It's okay to be eleven for a while and not take on adult stuff you can't solve anyway."

"I thought you said you knew me," I answer, half smiling to soften the mood a little. "You know I always take on adult stuff, and you know I can't just *be eleven*."

She shrugs. "Yeah. But you can try, at least?"

I look at Ava and get a sense that she's tired of me always worrying and taking on grown-up stuff. Maybe she wants me to just be more like Nina. I might lose the deli, and now I realize I might lose Ava, too.

We sit there in silence for a few more minutes until it's time to walk to lunch. I wonder if I can test out this regular eleven-year-old Ellie. Kind of like performing a part in a play or wearing a costume. Maybe I can shed worrier-about-adult-stuff Ellie and just focus on the kid part.

REGULAR WORRY-FREE, ELEVEN-YEAR-OLD ELLIE!

It seems kind of daunting but exciting at the same time.

I don't mention it to Ava. I'm just gonna see if she notices. It's a little experiment.

Nina, Aanya, Brynn, and Sally are already at the lunch table when Ava and I walk in. I wonder if Aanya knows about this restaurant row thing. I mean, it's her cousin's restaurant, but still. I want to talk to Aanya about her family's restaurant, but I can't at lunch since I don't want anyone else to overhear.

"So, you're literally never going to believe this, but you know that dream home contest on TV?" Sally asks.

Everyone nods.

"We won! We won a dream home in Florida. I don't know if we're keeping it because you can also just sell it and get the money and buy a house somewhere else, but we actually won!"

"Sally!" I yelp. "That is the most amazing thing everrrrrr."

Ava looks at me crooked already. My enthusiasm isn't usually this high, but also no one has ever won a home before!

"Right?" Sally says. "I am sooo excited. My mom enters contests all the time. So, yay, she finally won!"

"Can we go there with you? Girls trip! Mega sleepover! OMG!" I yell. "This is so amazing, Sal."

She giggles. "I told you I don't know if we're keeping it yet."

My face flashes a little red, embarrassed that I wasn't listening and that maybe I'm trying too hard to be all excited. I let the conversation go on at the lunch table. Brynn is talking about her grandma coming to visit and Nina is of course talking about her party.

"I am soooo excited for your party, Nina." I smile after a bite of turkey sandwich. "Like, so, so excited."

Ava makes eyes at me. She can tell I'm not talking like myself, not acting like myself. It feels like I'm playing a part in a play. I'll admit—it's kind of a little refreshing to be a little different form my usual self.

"It's going to be sooooo fun," I tell Nina, trying to sound all casual and chill.

"I'm so happy you're excited, Ellie." Nina's voice lifts at the end. I wonder if she thought I hated her this whole time. Well, not hate. But, that maybe I didn't necessarily like her so much.

"Totally!" I smile, open my bag of chips, and take one out. "Chip, anyone?" I offer the bag to the table.

Ava is still making eyes at me while Nina and I discuss days to get together to go shopping. But when lunch ends, I feel better than I've felt in a really, really long time.

This "trying on a new personality" thing is one of the best ideas I've ever had.

Chapter 13

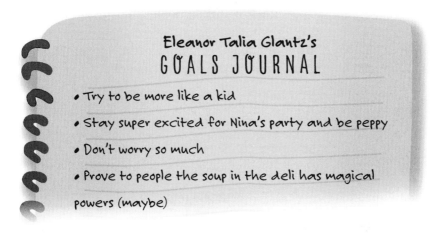

Eleanor Talia Glantz's
GOALS JOURNAL

- Try to be more like a kid
- Stay super excited for Nina's party and be peppy
- Don't worry so much
- Prove to people the soup in the deli has magical powers (maybe)

I get home from school, practically skipping because I feel great that Nina likes me, and great that I'm getting excited about her party, and also pretty pumped that Sally's mom won that dream home contest.

Maybe *operation try to be eleven* isn't the worst idea in the world. It really takes my mind off things and feels way more fun than my usual *too-grown-up-for-my-age Ellie* vibe.

I drop my backpack by the door, hang my coat on the hook, and head into the kitchen to grab my new favorite snack:

pretzels and a jar of peanut butter for dipping, plus a tall glass of lemonade with as many ice cubes as I can fit.

But as soon as I get into the kitchen, everything stops.

"Ellie, come sit," Mom says. Somehow Mabel and Anna are already there.

"What's going on?" I ask, a sinking feeling in my stomach that starts spiraling down to my ankles.

Mom sighs and fiddles with the fraying edge of a placemat. "I know you've been hearing things from Ava, and I know you're eavesdropping on our conversations around here. I should probably be better about talking when I know you're not asleep . . ." She pauses. "But listen, I want to be upfront with all of you. A restaurant developer has approached us about selling the deli. They want to revitalize all of restaurant row and sort of give it a little bit of a Times Square feel."

"Everyone knows Times Square is the worst part of Manhattan, but okay." Anna rolls her eyes.

"Anyway, they're giving us an offer that's pretty incredible. We'd be able to travel and pay for all of your college tuitions very easily. It would be very peaceful," Mom says.

"But then Lukshen won't be ours anymore," I say softly. "The deli is like our family member."

"Yeah, and you'll be bored in five minutes," Mabel adds. "So bored."

"Hate to say it, but Mabel's right," Anna adds. "She's seven and understands retirement."

"I know it's not the outcome any of us really wanted, but the deli has been struggling for a while, and finances are tight. I don't want to have to sell the house, and I don't want Bubbie and Zeyda to have to sell their house, either." Mom clears her throat. "They're getting older, and there will be medical expenses." She looks at us and then quickly looks away. "The developer is going to keep some of the menu items, some of the Lukshen flavor, of course. It won't all be gone."

"Okay, but it definitely won't be ours." I shake my head. "This is like giving away an elderly dog just because it's old and not as fun anymore."

Mom sniffles a little. "I know this a lot to take in, El."

"When is this happening?" I ask. "Is it a done deal?"

"It's not a done deal yet. There are terms to figure out. All sorts of things."

"Okay." I nod. "I need to finish homework."

Everyone looks at me a little crooked, like they weren't expecting this to be my response.

"You okay, El?" Mom asks, her voice soft.

I think back to the whole *try to be eleven thing* and how I can't possibly do that when the deli needs my help. I can *be eleven* sometimes, at lunch at school and with my friends, but now I need to take action.

"I'm fine. I need a week to prove to you this is a terrible mistake. And I will do that. Just promise me I have a week?"

Mom shakes her head, looking to Anna and Mabel for support, but they ignore her and stare at me, almost perplexed.

"Do I have a week?" I ask again.

"You have a week, Ellie. I don't know exactly when the meeting will take place. But please, remember you need to focus on schoolwork and your own life. I didn't tell you this so you'd take over and feel it's your responsibility."

"I know," I reply and get up from the table.

I need a week. That's it.

I already have the idea to prove that Lukshen Deli needs to stay the way it is. Exactly the way it is, and that it can thrive and be better than it has ever been before.

Later that night, I'm at my desk doing homework when Ava bursts into my room. I hadn't even heard the doorbell ring.

"Ellie." She plops down on my bed. "We need to talk. What was up with you at lunch today?"

"I was just trying to be more fun." I shrug.

"Are you in a competition with me for who can be better friends with Nina?" Ava asks, arms folded across her chest. "If so, that's really weird."

"Ava! What? No! I was just trying to be fun, and a little more like an eleven-year-old." I pause. "I just want to be fun and nice and not so grumpy and anxious all the time."

"Okay." Ava looks down at my carpet. "I guess that makes sense." She leans back against my pillows and stays quiet, and I start to think she's fallen asleep. I go back to my math worksheet and leave her there, snoozing away.

A few moments later, she asks. "So, what else is going on?"

"Um. Nothing. Just trying to finish homework." I talk with my back to her. I purposefully avoid mentioning my one-week plan to keep the deli. I don't want to be bogged down with adult stuff again. It's all part of my mission to be a fun, normal, easygoing kid, especially around Ava.

"I should do that, too, I guess." Ava says, still lying down on my bed.

I start to realize something's up with Ava and it may not be about the whole Nina thing or my new vibe.

"You okay, Aves?" I ask her.

"Eh."

"Eh?"

"I think my mom is in love."

I spin around on my bungee chair to turn to face her. "Really?"

"Yeah, she's acting all weird lately. Singing to herself. And she's had a lot of meetings, but I don't think they're really meetings. I think they're dates. And I just have a hunch she's in love."

"This happened before, though," I remind her. "Remember that time in fourth grade, she took you to the fair with that person?"

"Yeah."

"Don't stress, Aves. You may be making this up. And maybe she'll be in love with someone you like."

"Maybe. It's all ick, ya know?"

"Definitely all ick. Parents and love is ick in general."

"I'm used to it being just my mom and me, and I get a little weirded out thinking about someone new joining my world," Ava continues. "And if someone joins my world with my dad, too. Then I really don't know what I'll do. Too many world-joiners."

"I totally get that," I add. "Any change is weird. And this is a big change. But it hasn't happened yet. No sense stressing about something before it's even happened."

"Ellie!" she yells. "Who are you right now? That's basically your number one thing—stressing about something before it's happened."

"I know." I giggle. "Which is why I don't want you to do it! I want you to learn from my mistakes."

I get up from my desk, walk over to my bed, and put an arm around her. "Don't worry, Aves. I'm here for you. Today, tomorrow, yesterday, FOR LIFE."

Ava cracks up. "I know, I know. But I appreciate the reminder."

The conversation with my mom about the deli is taking up at least half my thoughts at the moment and I want to bring it up with Ava, but she has so much on her brain that I feel like I can't. Not right now, at least.

After Ava leaves, I start mapping out a specific plan. I write down notes in my goals journal and I really feel like all of this is going to work. It's a confidence I can't explain. It's like the soup; I just know it's magic.

I think about Lukshen starting a minyan. A place where people can come together. Not only for food, but for companionship, too, and not only good times, but hard ones as well.

I'm about to start emailing local rabbis when I realize I'm going about this all wrong. They're not going to listen to a kid.

I have an even better idea.

It may take a little longer, but not too long, still within my one-week timeframe.

It does involve me going to the deli every day after school, though.

Chapter 14

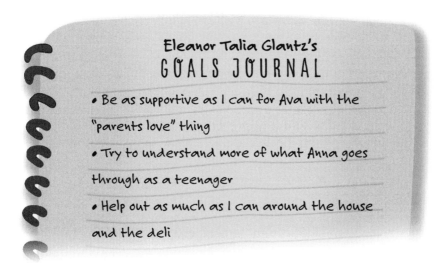

Eleanor Talia Glantz's
GOALS JOURNAL
• Be as supportive as I can for Ava with the
"parents love" thing
• Try to understand more of what Anna goes
through as a teenager
• Help out as much as I can around the house
and the deli

I kind of feel like I'm living a double life.

It's not as extreme as that sounds, of course, but it's close.

Here's how it goes: at lunch I'm all chatty, normal, regular sixth-grade girl, Ellie Glantz.

Then, after school, I'm Ellie Glantz, Lukshen Deli Reviver.

I go to the deli, make a lot of wishes on the soup, try to observe everything I can, and help out as much as I can.

And, of course, I wait for Norman to come in again. It's Sunday, and I only have four days left. Lukshen Deli is closed on Saturdays, because it's Shabbat, which is the Jewish day of rest. Every week, all Kosher businesses are closed from Friday at sundown to Saturday at sundown. I love Shabbat. Yesterday, I got to hang out with my family at home and not worry about the deli for a minute.

Norman's gotta come in today. Otherwise, I'm going to have to go to my backup plan, which is looking through Bubbie's old address book and finding his number or hopefully his email address.

"Ellie, my love, am I forcing you to come here every day?" Bubbie asks me, smoothing out the top of a tray of coleslaw. Her voice sounds a little more tired today, not as energetic as usual. It worries me but I push it away. She's here. She's fine. "I love having your company, but you shouldn't feel obligated to come here, you know."

"I know, Bub. I like being here."

"Sure?"

"Yes, I'm sure."

I sit by the window and pray that Norman comes here. Then I crack myself up because I'm an eleven-year-old girl praying an old man shows up at the deli.

A few minutes later, a string of customers come in. Mostly older people getting off the train and grabbing dinner before they head home. Some picking up for themselves and some for families. I want to say to each and every one of them: "The deli might close! Soon you might not have the privilege of seeing my Bubbie every day! Help me!" But I don't.

The more time passes, the more ridiculous I feel. Yet I know my plan will work. I just know it.

Eventually, I have to leave my little perch by the front window because I desperately must pee. I run as fast as I can to the bathroom in the back and pee as quickly as possible so I don't miss Norman if he comes in.

I finish washing my hands and rush to the front of the deli.

Oh my goodness! Norman!

He's at the counter, schmoozing with Bubbie as she packs up a fried chicken and some containers of soup.

"Um, hi, Norman," I say, all casual sounding. "Can I talk to you for a second?"

"Ellie?" Bubbie asks, perplexed. I nudge to her that I have it under control.

Norman follows me off to the side a little, looking at me the way many adults do when I try to talk to them, sort of amused and confused at the same time.

"So, Norman, first of all, I'm really sorry for your loss."

He nods. "Thank you, Ellie."

"When you came in for minyan the other night, a major idea came to me, and I realized that I need to help make it happen." I pause. "I think we should hold a daily minyan here. For the community, I mean. And people can get dinner if they want, or just stay and schmooze. Mourning is really lonely and isolating, and we can be here for people."

Norman steps back a little.

"Wow. I'm kind of speechless. But you're right."

"Will you help me make this happen? Help me reach out to the rabbis in town?"

He shrugs. "I can try."

"Oh, and don't mention anything to my Bubbie yet," I whisper and look back over my shoulder to make sure she's not listening.

"Well, I don't know about that. I think we should loop her in, no?"

"Not yet. Please. Promise me?"

"Okay." He smiles. "I'll let you know what happens."

"Thank you so much," I whisper. "Remember. Not a word of this to Bubbie."

He nods and smiles and walks ahead of me, back to the counter. I hang back a little, feeling mostly pleased with this tiny bit of progress. We don't have a ton of time, but hopefully we have enough.

Sometimes all it takes is a tiny little burst of something to make you feel inspired to keep going, to maybe even amp up your efforts a little.

I run to the back office, grab my phone, and video-call Ava.

"Aves. Hi."

She giggles. "You seem like you're up to something. What is it?"

"Okay. So." I take a deep breath. My mind is racing a million miles a minute and I feel like my voice is going to start racing, too. "Remember when you told me about Terri? Who owns the Marlborough Lake PR agency?"

Ava's face turns bright red, almost like I just walked in on her in a public bathroom stall when she was in the middle of a stomach bug. Gross, but true.

"You okay?"

She's silent then, staring into space like she's about to say something so extreme. My heart pounds, the seconds tick by, and it feels like forever before words come out of her mouth again.

"Ellie. Terri is the person my mom is in love with, I think." She pauses. "I thought you knew that."

"Um, what? No." I scan my brain to see if she told me the person's name but I'm ninety-nine percent sure she didn't. "Oh. I don't think you told me the person."

"Yeah. I think they really are in love," Ava continues. "They've been friends forever and ever. And now I think it's more than friends. They talk on the phone for hours at night, and no one talks on the phone anymore! And there were flowers on the table today with a card that just had a heart and the name Terri."

"Wow," is all I can manage to say. Adult romance is just not something I really want to think about.

"Yeah." Ava shakes her head. "Anyway, putting my mom's love life aside for a second, and fingers crossed *forever* because I hate to talk about it. What do you need?"

I smile. Clearly Ava's struggling with the whole her-mom-and-Terri thing and yet she still wants to help me. Is there any better friend than Ava Naomi Milkin?

I don't think so.

"So, when we talked a bit ago, you mentioned the PR agency, and I'm hoping she can whip something up really fast for the deli. And also for free? I'm kind of on a time crunch here . . ."

"Oh, Ellie. You're one of a kind."

Ava bursts out laughing and then I do, too, and I don't even know what we're laughing about.

"But seriously, can you ask her? Or can you ask your mom to ask her? And say it's a giant favor. And say we'll repay her in pickles—half sour or sour, her choice. And say she can eat free at Lukshen Deli for the rest of her life!"

"Okay, don't go that far." Ava widens her eyes. "I'll talk to my mom. But I am only doing this for you!" She yells the last part. "That's how much I love you, Eleanor!"

"Oh, ew. Don't call me Eleanor."

"I can call you whatever I want if I'm helping you."

I shake my head. "Okay. Fine. Thank you."

I hear my Bubbie calling me from the front of the deli, so I hang up with Ava and leave the office.

When I get to the counter, Bubbie's slumped over, leaning on the counter like she's unable to stand up.

"Bub?" I ask, softly. Something is definitely not right.

"I don't feel well all of a sudden." She chokes out the words, slowly, almost like they're boulders coming out of her mouth. "I called your mother. She's on her way."

"Bub." I freeze in place, unable to move. Should I call my mom first? Call 911? But Mom is already on the way . . .

I look over at the soup on the stove.

I don't want to leave Bubbie's side to stare into the pot, so I try and do my whole wishing ritual from over here, as quickly as possible, while hitting the contact for my mom's phone at the same time.

Even though I'm not standing directly over the stove, I'm still really hoping my matzo ball wishes can work. I think it can. I'm close enough.

Please let Bubbie be okay. Please let Bubbie be okay. Please let Bubbie be okay. This is really all that matters. Please let Bubbie be okay.

"Ellie, I'm outside the deli," Mom says, and then quickly hangs up.

She rushes in and puts her arm around Bubbie. Thankfully Bubbie is still able to walk. Mom gets her to the car, quickly locks up, and I tell myself to be supportive and understanding, but I have no idea what to do.

I don't want to go to the hospital with them now—or ever.

Hospitals scare me. The smell, the beeping, the way the doctors shuffle around. I hate all of it. But we're going.

"It's going to be okay, Bub," I say from the back seat, even though I'm totally making that up and have no idea if it's actually going to be okay. It just feels like the right thing to say in the moment.

She doesn't say much in response, just a sort of groany moany combination sound, and then she rests her head against the window. I don't even know what hurts—her stomach? Is it hard for her to breathe? Is it her heart?

I feel terrible that I don't know. Those are details I should have paid attention to.

We do the valet parking. Mom basically throws the keys at the guy and doesn't wait for the ticket. I lag behind a second so he hands it to me, and I shove it in my jeans pocket. We rush into the emergency room. Before I can even blink or understand what's happening, Mom and Bubbie are ushered back to a room, and I'm left alone on the icky peach vinyl couches in the waiting area.

I look around at everyone, wishing I wasn't alone in here, wishing I wasn't here at all, and praying harder than I've ever prayed that they figure out whatever is going on and that Bubbie is okay.

I quickly text Ava.

> Bub is in the hospital. We had to rush here. Don't know whats going on :(

She writes back right away.

> Oh no! Do you want me to come?
> My mom can drive me.

It's okay, but thank you. I'll keep you updated.

Ok. Xoxoxoxo

I look over at the magazine rack, debating taking one, but can't even bring myself to get up. I am frozen in this seat with fear. What if something really bad is happening to Bubbie? Something so bad she never fully recovers? And then she's never able to pick me up and drive me to the deli again, or make the soup or the matzo balls or the brisket sandwiches? What if she's too weak to even be able to scoop our famous coleslaw into containers?

And holidays? What if she can never make a Rosh Hashanah round challah again? What if she can never make her famous mushroom kugel for Passover?

It's all too much. My mind is swirling with *what ifs*. Terrible, horrible, the worst ever *what ifs*. My brain goes to dark places, too—stop, stop, stop, stop.

I can't. I can't think this. I won't let myself. I refuse.

I stay there, on that icky seat, for what feels like another three hours, but I've lost track of time, and I wonder why Dad isn't coming, or Anna, or anyone, really. Do they know I'm alone in this waiting room? I look at my phone again to see if anyone has texted, but nope. Nothing.

So, I just stay where I am, holding my head in my hands, counting the little green dots on the linoleum tile, trying not to breathe in the bleachy lemon floor cleaner that stings my nostrils.

"El, come on," says a voice suddenly. It's Mom, brushing some sweaty strands of hair away from her forehead. She catches me totally off guard, and I startle and jerk forward. "Bubbie's been admitted. We can go to her room."

Admitted? For college that's a good thing, but for a hospital it's a terrible thing.

I want to ask Mom questions, but my throat is dry. I can't even seem to form complete thoughts, so I definitely don't think I'll be able to get words to come out of my mouth.

We take the elevator and then down the hallway a little bit until we reach Bubbie's room. She's there, in the bed, in a very drowsy state, connected to an IV and other monitors. It seems like a million machines are beeping all at the same time. I don't know what the beeps mean. I don't know if they're bad beeps or good beeps. Something tells me all beeps like this are bad beeps.

"Oh dear," Mom says, walking over to her. She pulls an ugly green chair close to Bubbie's bed, sits down on the very edge of it, and just sort of stares at her, rubbing her arm.

In my head, I want to tell her to relax, tell her it's all going to be okay, but I still can't get words to come out.

"Hi, dolls," Bubbie says, sounding weak.

She's able to speak, though! That's gotta be a good sign, right? A great sign, actually!

A few minutes later, Dad gets here, finally, and Zeyda is with him. I guess Anna and Mabel stayed home. All of a sudden, I'm overwhelmed with jealousy. I want to be home. Or maybe I don't want to be home, but I know I don't want to be here. I don't want to be anywhere. I can't think of a single place where it

would be good to be, with Bubbie in the hospital. Even if I were on the most beautiful tropical island with fruity umbrella drinks and a perfect heated pool with waterslides, I still wouldn't be happy if Bubbie was sick in this bed.

She can't stay like this. She has to be okay. She has to.

A doctor comes in and then asks if she can talk to Zeyda and Mom outside. Dad goes with them, and I'm suddenly so freaked out being alone in here with Bubbie. She's only half awake, and we're not really chatting, and what if something happens to her while I'm in here? What would I do?

I have to leave the room. And then I feel guilty for leaving because I think I should be a supportive, nice, kind granddaughter and stay with her. But I can't. I'm too scared. I hate seeing her like this. This isn't Bubbie. Not at all.

"Be right back," I say, even though her eyes are closed now, and I think she fell asleep. I blow her a kiss from the door and whisper, "Love you, Bub." Then I walk out into the hallway and stand with my back against the wall.

I'm too stressed to even eavesdrop on my parents and Zeyda right now. I don't even want to eavesdrop because I don't want to hear or know what they're saying.

Instead, I stand there in the hallway and try to see what one of the nurses is doing on her computer. I think she's playing solitaire. I convince myself that nothing can be that urgent if a nurse on this hospital floor has time to play a computer game.

There. I calmed myself down.

For a moment at least.

A few minutes later, Zeyda and my parents walk back into the room, and I follow them. My eyes move back and forth from them to Bubbie and then to the loud-ticking clock above the TV.

Zeyda goes over to Bubbie's bed and kisses her forehead.

"We can stay longer," Mom says.

"Go home," Bubbie mumbles. "I'm okay."

I'm relieved to hear her say this, even though I'm not totally sure if she's being truthful or not.

Zeyda and my parents come get me, and we walk into the already-too-chilly-for-fall night. I kind of wish I had a warmer coat with me. The cold zips through my body so fast that my teeth start chattering.

"Zeyda, I think you should sleep over at our house," I say so everyone can hear me. "You shouldn't be alone tonight."

"Oh, Ellie." He laughs, even though nothing in the whole world feels funny right now. "I'll be okay."

"Come on, please, it'll be like a real, official sleepover. You can have my bed. I'll sleep on the couch. Please."

I look to both of my parents and they're doing a thing where they communicate with facial expressions, even though I'm not so sure how well they're communicating in the dark of the Marlborough Lake Hospital parking lot.

"Dad, Ellie's right," Mom says and puts an arm around him. "Come home with us, please."

Zeyda nods reluctantly. "Whatever works for all of you."

For a second, I feel all cheerful, thinking about Zeyda sleeping over and eating cheesy eggs with him tomorrow morning, forgetting for a moment why we're here, and even where we are, and the whole situation altogether.

I think our brains like to do that, to kind of give us a break sometimes. I'm not a scientist or a neurologist or anything but I just have a hunch that it's true.

Our brains can't feel any one emotion all the time—anger or sadness or worry—and we can't focus on one stressful thing all the time, either.

So without us even knowing it, our brains give us breaks.

It's pretty amazing when you think about it.

On the car ride back to my house with just Mom and Zeyda in the car (Dad drives himself), we all sit quietly.

"Is Bubbie going to be okay?" I ask finally, when I can't take the silence anymore.

"Of course!" Zeyda says like it's not even a question.

I decide not to ask anything else and just go with that for now and believe him. That's the only thought my brain wants to have, anyway.

I wish we were listening to music or a podcast or something because I want to distract myself. I'm worried about Bubbie. And I'm worried about the deli. And I'm also anxious to hear about Norman's progress, and Ava's, too, with Terri and her mom and the whole thing.

And then I wonder if the one-week timeline even applies anymore.

Now I feel like my brain needs to take another break or it's going to explode.

EGG CASSEROLE

INGREDIENTS
1½ cups croutons
1 cup grated cheddar cheese
6 eggs, beaten
1¾ cup milk
Salt and pepper to taste

INSTRUCTIONS
1. Butter the pan.

2. Put the croutons and cheese in the pan.

3. Combine the rest of the ingredients and add to the pan.

4. Bake for 30 to 45 minutes at 325 degrees.

Chapter 15

Zeyda sleeps over, and Mom makes her cheesy egg casserole for breakfast the next morning. We all sit at the table and eat together before school and it sort of feels like a holiday or something. But it's actually the exact opposite with Bubbie in the hospital. Still, if you only looked at our plates, and all of us together in the kitchen, you'd think everything was really awesome. Like it was a celebration, almost. Maybe that's part of Bubbie's magic, too.

I force myself to nibble a few bites of breakfast, but my stomach is too twisted with worry about Bubbie to really eat much. My anxiety always seems to settle in the middle of my body, and when I'm nervous, I just can't think about food.

During lunch at school, I still really don't have an appetite. So I'm taken aback when Nina shouts "Guys!" across the table, and all the other tables around us turn to see what's happening. "My party is coming up so soon! Can you even believe it?"

Aanya smiles. "I can't wait!"

"I'm soooo excited," I say, putting on my other Ellie personality, trying to think about literally anything else besides Bubbie lying in a hospital bed right now. It seems to be the only thing my brain wants to focus on, though. Like even if my thoughts move away from it for a second, they just jump right back there.

Nina goes on and on about the mini hot dogs and all the foods she's getting and this fortune teller who's coming. Then Ava taps me on the shoulder. She must have noticed I was really quiet on our walk to the bus this morning. "Ellie, can we talk over there for a second?"

The whole table stares at us and I start sweating.

"Um, sure."

We walk to the side of the cafeteria near the double doors to the courtyard.

"What's up?" I ask her, all cheery, still with my other Ellie personality on.

"First of all, how's Bubbie?" she asks.

I shrug. "I don't have a new update. They're still doing tests, I think."

"Well, my mom says Marlborough Lake Hospital is one of the best medical centers in the country," Ava says, trying to be reassuring. "So, your Bub is in good hands."

"I hope so."

"Okay, second of all, I talked to Terri."

"And?"

"And she wants to help! Maybe because she's in love with my mom, but also maybe because she's just a nice person. Anyway. She's going to come up with a whole plan, nothing too overwhelming to start, but she said she can have her assistant manage the social media for us for now. And remember when you had the idea about Jerry the mailman working there, and that friend of Anna's? Whatever happened with that?"

"Oh yeah! I don't even know. I need to follow up on that."

Ava thinks for a moment. "Well, if you can get them on board for deliveries, Terri said she can help you get set up with all the food delivery apps in the area. She just did it for that place Taco Taco down the street."

My head starts to feel very tight, almost like there are too many thoughts clotting it up and soon it's going to wobble off my neck and fall to the floor.

I think this might be what they mean when you can sense an anxiety attack coming on. It feels like how they described it in that pamphlet from Nurse Wilkinson. There are so many moving pieces all at once.

"Ellie? You okay?"

"Not really," I mumble. "Right now, I feel overwhelmed."

I slump down to the floor against the wall of the cafeteria with all of the lunch noises swirling around me like cartoon spirals.

"Okay, one thing at a time, El." Ava slides down the wall, too, and sits next to me. A second later, I realize we're sitting side by side on the gross cafeteria floor, but I'm too overwhelmed to even worry about that.

Ava pipes up. "My dad has already started designing the website, free of charge! We'll just have Terri start the social media stuff. She's really savvy with it and obviously she's eaten at Lukshen a million times." Ava pauses and sort of strokes my shoulder in this awkward but also kind of nice way. "She said it's a labor of love."

I look up and smile. "That's good, then."

"Listen, Ellie," Ava says. "Lunch is almost over. But trust that I'm looking out for you, and I want to help, and it'll all be okay."

I nod.

"I mean it."

I really hope she's right.

After school, I yell through our front screen door that I'm going to Ava's, and then Ava and I walk into her house, where we find her mom and Terri at the kitchen table. Maybe I'm reading into it because of what Ava said, but I kind of think they're in love, too. They're sitting so close to each other with permanent smiles on, and it doesn't even look like they're doing anything fun. They're just smiling because they're together.

"Just the people I wanted to see!" Terri yells, clearing some papers off the chairs so there's room for us to sit down. "This deli rebrand is going to be so incredible. And I know it's kind of just an experiment and maybe a little out of the ordinary that I haven't checked with your mom or Bubbie yet, Ellie. But even still, I'm all for encouraging young girls' entrepreneurial spirit . . . so here we go." She pauses. "Ready?"

Wow, she really has a lot to say. Ava's mom is just sitting back in her chair, smiling with a heart-eyes expression on her face.

"I'm ready!" I smile.

"Me too," Ava adds.

Terri opens up her computer and shows us some logos she's designed and the placement of Lukshen's menu on this online delivery platform. It all looks really, really good.

"Dad's designing the website," Ava adds, proudly. I feel a pinch of awkwardness for Terri, but she doesn't seem fazed by it.

"Wonderful," Ava's mom says. "What a team we have here!"

"So basically, I'll need the official go-ahead from your parents to launch all of this, Ellie, and I imagine Doug will, too." She smiles. I guess it makes sense that she knows Ava's dad. They've all lived in Marlborough Lake a really long time. She turns to me. "How's your Bubbie doing?"

I smile, comforted by the fact that we live in such a small town where people care about others. "I think she's doing better, but I should go home, actually, and check in," I say, feeling anxious all of a sudden, like I don't know what's going on. Instead of stewing in my worries, I might as well see what's up. I'm learning that it really helps me to take action instead of just sitting in my anxiety. "I'll come right back and then I'll have a better idea of who you should talk to."

"Sounds good, Ellie." Terri smiles. When I'm almost out the door, I overhear her say, "That's a girl who knows what she wants and won't give up until she gets it!"

My whole body warms up when she says that. A girl who knows what she wants and won't give up until she gets it is exactly who I want to be. I'm so glad that Terri sees me that way.

I walk in the house and Mom is on the phone. Of course, I don't go into the kitchen right away. I stand in the little archway between the den and kitchen and try to listen.

"Right, right. Of course. Thank you so much. Yes, I'll be there to sign everything and bring her home as soon as you tell me it's time." Pause. "I understand. I can't thank you enough, Dr. Berks. This feels like the best course of action for everyone. Thank you again."

I feel my face smiling without even realizing I'm doing it. This must be about Bubbie! It has to be good news! I hope it means she's coming home.

"Hi, Mom," I say, pretending I didn't hear anything, taking a mini bottle of iced tea out of the fridge.

"Hi, El." The tone of her voice is tired sounding, but also sort of relaxed, calm, maybe even a tiny bit pleased?

"How's Bub?" I ask, my heart pounding from overhearing that phone call just now and from all the others worries swirling around my head.

"Better, thank goodness!" Mom smiles. "Good enough to come home, at least, and we can follow up with her doctors and everything later."

"Best news ever!" I reach out to high-five my mom. At first, she's confused, but then she sort of lopsided, half high-fives me back.

I sit down at the table and realize I need to tell her about the Terri thing, and kind of quickly because I need to get back over there.

"So, you know Terri? Ava's mom's, um, friend?" My cheeks flash hot, realizing I don't know how to describe her.

"Of course I know Terri." She sits back in her chair and takes a sip of the coffee that's definitely been sitting out since this morning.

"Soooo . . . she's done all this rebranding for Lukshen! Set us up on the Marlborough Lake restaurant delivery platform, logos, all this stuff," I say, spitting a little because I'm so excited and my words are coming out so fast. "And Ava's dad is putting the finishing touches on the website."

"Really?" Mom's eyes bulge. "You did all this? You talked to Terri?"

I giggle for a second. "Well, Ava handled the Terri part. And the Doug part. But yeah, I mean, yeah, I helped! Terri's over at Ava's right now. Come with me, and you can see it all and approve it and we can get started."

"Ellie, this is a lot to start with. We don't have delivery people lined up yet."

"Cybil and Jerry!"

"Jerry the mail carrier?" Mom looks at me sideways.

"He needs a new line of work, remember?"

"Right. Yes." Mom pauses to think a minute. "Wow, El, you've really thought of everything."

I half smile. "Well, I don't want the deli to go out of business, and I don't want to have to move, but I also don't want to lose it entirely to this developer, either. I had to take matters into my own hands." I link arms with her. "Come with me, just come see."

Mom exhales, and I think it's with relief. Relief about Bubbie, I think, mostly. So much that she's willing to go along with this and see what happens. Sometimes you need a really scary thing to happen to make you appreciate all the other stuff and sort of help you keep an open mind.

But this Bubbie scare only proves even more that we need to save Lukshen! We need to preserve it for as long as we can, because we don't know how long Bubbie and Zeyda will be around. Nothing is certain. I need to make sure we have a book of all the recipes, everything preserved. We need to keep as many things the same as we can.

We walk over to Ava's together and my whole chest feels like it's filled with marshmallows, like I'm almost floating with my feet a little bit above the ground.

"Hi, Terri, hi, Raina, hi, Ava." Mom blows kisses to all of them at the table. I haven't seen her this relaxed in months and months. Maybe she's been worrying about Bubbie for way longer than any of us even realized.

"Hello, Mara," Ava's mom and Terri say at the same time.

My mom sits down. Terri folds her hands on the table and then just starts talking. "First of all, how's your mom?"

"Doing much better, thank goodness." Mom smiles.

"That's wonderful." Terri pauses. "Second of all, your daughter is a budding entrepreneur. You know this, yes?"

Mom looks at me and laughs for a second. "That seems accurate, yes."

"And we all adore Lukshen Deli. Really adore. Cannot imagine Marlborough Lake without it, and I know there's the talk about the restaurant row and all of that, but Lukshen *is* the Einhorn-Glantz family. No way around it." She smiles. "So, I've offered to help, and I like what I've done so far. I hope you will, too. We can test the waters with Marlborough Lake Eats, the online platform most of the restaurants are using." She pauses. "Anyway, I'm talking too much. Take a look. See what you think."

Terri pushes the computer over to my mom. She scrolls through all the pages while I peer over her shoulder, so close I'm almost resting my chin on the ruffles of her sweatshirt.

"Wow, this is incredible stuff." Mom looks over at Terri. "Really, really good. You just whipped this up?"

"Well, I had some help." Terri winks at me. "You like it?"

"I love it!" Mom pulls me in for a sideways cuddle. "Listen, I promised Ellie she could have a week to show me what she envisions so we can see about drumming up business and keeping the deli going . . ." My mom exhales. "And with my mother in the hospital, our deadline has been extended, anyway. So, let's get this set up. El, we'll talk to Cybil and Jerry about being delivery people and then we can go from there."

"Wonderful!" Terri exclaims. "To make matters easier, I'll work with Doug on setting up the website with this logo and we'll work together. There'll be a place to sign up for Lukshen Loyalty on there."

"Lukshen Loyalty!" my mom shouts. "I just love it!"

I look over at Ava. It must feel like a relief that Terri and her dad can get along. Probably a relief to her mom, too.

"This is amazing!" I yell because I'm overcome with happiness.

"We are amazing!" Ava high-fives me from across the table.

"Yes, we are!"

Mom continues chatting with Ava's mom and Terri. Ava and I run upstairs to her room.

"Oh my goodness, this is happening. We are doing this! We are saving this deli!" Ava swings me around like we're at some kind of impromptu dance party.

"Yes! I can't even believe it. I feel speechless."

Ava laughs. "Wow, that really never happens to you."

"I know!" I pause, remembering something. "Oh, also, I didn't tell you about this minyan thing. It's another major idea I have for the deli."

"Minyan? Wow. I want to hear."

"We need snacks first," I insist. "We always needs snacks first."

"Agree. One hundred percent agree."

Ava and I hang out the rest of the day and I tell her all about the minyan thing. We make a bunch of "at the deli" playlists and dream up different events that people might want to host there.

Later that night, I'm brushing my teeth before bed when I hear my parents whispering to each other in their bedroom. The door is mostly closed, but it's open a crack and I don't understand why they always talk just loud enough for me to hear them. It's like they almost want me to always overhear them, somehow.

"I'm not sure I prepared the girls enough for what it'll be like with my mother home now," Mom says in a hushed tone. "She's okay, just weaker than she was before. And that might be a hard adjustment . . ."

"You didn't tell them anything," Dad says in a jokey way, and laughs. "So how could they be prepared?"

"You know what I mean."

"Mar, it'll be okay. We'll figure it out as we go."

"Sure?" she asks.

"Sure."

They don't say anything else after that, and I find myself wishing I hadn't overheard it. I push it away. Bubbie's okay, but weak, and we can definitely handle that.

I take deep calming breaths, like Nurse Wilkinson said to do, and I force myself not to worry.

Worrying never helps. I need to remember that.

MEAT LOAF

INGREDIENTS

1½ pounds ground beef

¾ cups oats

2 eggs, beaten

2 teaspoons salt

¼ cup chopped onions

¼ teaspoon pepper

1 cup tomato juice

INSTRUCTIONS

1. Combine all the ingredients thoroughly and pack firmly into a loaf pan.

2. Bake at 350 degrees for 1 hour.

3. Let stand 5 minutes before slicing.

Chapter 16

*B*ubbie comes home from the hospital the next day. My parents go to pick her up while Zeyda and I are at the deli. I go to help him, of course, but also to wait for Norman. He's supposed to get back to me today about the minyan plan, and then hopefully we can just get started. Of course, no one but Ava knows that I'm actually pursuing this. Not yet, anyway.

"Ellie, can you help refill the ketchups? Have you noticed more people have been coming in to actually eat here lately?" Zeyda asks. Mom has stepped in to do some of the cooking while Bubbie is out, but she's just not as fast as her.

"Yes and yes!" I grab the big jug of ketchup from the back and bring it over to the tables using this little funnel thing to make sure none of it spills. "Why do you think that is?"

Zeyda looks up from the counter. "Not sure, really, but it's great! Is there some kind of deli trend going on?"

I crack up. Deli trend. I mean, I guess it's possible.

Zeyda says he's going to make some phone calls in the office, but I know his secret. Sometimes he takes a little snooze back there, leans back in the rolling desk chair and conks out for a bit. He doesn't know I know this, so I just nod and say okay when he says he has some "calls and paperwork to take care of."

I'm behind the stove, standing over the pot of soup, about to make a wish, when I get a video call from Ava. I hit ignore and stare into the pot.

Masterful brothy powers, please let Bubbie be her usual self when she gets home. Please don't let her be sick or weak. Or even if she is, let her recover really fast and eventually get back to her Bubbie self.

After my wish, I call Ava back.

"Ellie!" she yells as soon as she answers. "We need to decide on Halloween costumes, like, immediately."

"I know, I agree." I look at the calendar.

Halloween isn't a Jewish holiday. There's a Jewish holiday in the spring called Purim where we wear costumes, and I kind of think it's more fun because you get to use a noisemaker in temple whenever the bad guy, Haman, is mentioned. Last year, I dressed up as Queen Esther, who saved the Jewish people from Haman a long, long time ago. But Halloween is big in Marlborough Lakes, and I think it's special that I get to dress up twice a year.

"We also need to decide if we are doing a group thing with everyone else. Or just us?" Ava's voice is high-pitched and squeaky, and she talks really, really fast.

"I'll come over after I get back from the deli, and we'll figure everything out," I explain. "I'm waiting for Norman to come talk about the minyan. And I'm waiting for Jerry to call back, plus Anna's going to find out from Cybil if she wants to do the deliveries. And Bubbie's coming home from the hospital today!" I nervous-laugh. "A lot going on here!"

"There's a lot going on everywhere!" Ava screams. "Okay, hanging up, bye."

A minute later, the deli landline phone rings.

"Hello? It's Jerry," the voice booms.

"Jerry! Hi! It's Ellie."

"Ellie! Wonderful!"

There's a second or two of awkward silence and then Jerry says, "I hear you need a delivery driver . . . I'm here for you."

"Really?" I yelp, my heart expanding and expanding with the feeling that things may actually work out.

"Of course! What else am I doing?" Jerry laughs.

"Wonderful. Thank you so much, Jerry. I'll get back to you about when to start and how the process works and everything."

"Looking forward to it," Jerry says. "Bye, Ellie."

I lean over onto the counter and look around, taking it all in. I know we're just at the beginning, and it's unclear how all of these new plans will work, but I still feel good about it.

"Ellie. Where is Ellie?" Zeyda sings. "Where are you?"

"I'm here!" I burst out from behind the counter. "And I have news!"

"News?" Zeyda's eyes crinkle around the corners.

"Yes! Jerry is in to do the deliveries. Anna is checking with Cybil, we're making so much progress . . ." I lean over and hug him.

"Wow. I love this tenacity! Determination! I love all of it. But, retiring could also be nice . . . we could go on cruises, trips to Paris." Zeyda widens his eyes. "This developer is offering quite a nice deal."

"Zeyda, no. Not yet. Maybe some time down the road, but Lukshen is part of our family. We can't just sign it away."

Zeyda shrugs. "We'll have to see what Bubbie says. You know I'm not in charge."

I laugh. "Yeah. I know."

A string of customers starts coming in and Stacy helps them behind the counter while Zeyda schmoozes with all of them: a mom coming in to buy platters for her book club, an older couple picking up sandwiches to take with them on the drive to visit their grandchildren in New Hampshire, a man coming off the train picking up the family special for dinner tonight. Bubbie's really the schmoozer who knows all of them, knows their stories, cares to hear what they have to say. But Zeyda tries; he knows that's part of the magic of Lukshen, too.

If a restaurant developer buys this place, that'll all be lost.

I'm finishing a math worksheet at one of the tables when Anna and Cybil burst into the deli, laughing like I've never heard them laugh before. Heads thrown back, cackling, unable to catch their breath, almost falling onto the floor a few times.

"What's going on?" I ask them.

"It's a long story, Ellie. I'll tell you later, though," Anna says. "Cybil is here, ready to be our delivery girl!"

"Hi, Cybil." I smile. "That's awesome, but we're not going to be officially on the site until tomorrow. Mom has to sign some forms."

"That's cool," Cybil says. "I'm super excited to be able to do this."

"I might go with her for deliveries," Anna adds. "Especially if the Hackley twins order . . ."

They laugh again, almost like they might actually fall over, but then they get themselves together.

"It's great that you care so much, Ellie," Cybil says, walking over to me. It feels like my heart could explode with happiness. This is Anna's best friend saying I'm great! And before that trip to the stationery store, I really thought Anna hated me and we'd never be close again.

It's amazing how things can and do change. Sometimes for the better. I need to remember that.

"Zeyda," Anna calls out. "Can you make Cybil and me a turkey sandie with coleslaw and Russian dressing?"

Sandie? Okay, so there's still an obnoxiousness to Anna, but she's definitely better than she was before.

"Ooh, yum," Cybil says. "That sounds so good right now."

"Coming right up!"

Zeyda makes them the sandwich in pretty much record time.

"This is so good." Anna talks with her mouth full. "You don't understand how starving I was."

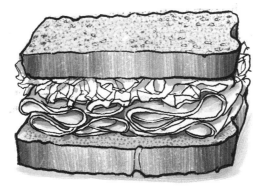

"Um, yes I do," Cybil answers. "I was the same level of starving."

I go behind the counter to neaten the piles of to-go containers and napkins before Norman comes, and then the deli phone rings again.

"Hi. Ellie? It's Terri."

"Oh, hi! How are you?"

"I'm great. We're all set up on the delivery platform. I just wondered if we could have a meeting with Jerry and Cybil to go over it all. I found us an option where we can select our delivery people. Sometimes the apps have their own drivers, but I wanted to make sure we had a spot for Jerry and Cybil." She pauses. "I spoke to your mom and Bubbie, and they're on board, but I want to make sure you're included. When are you free?"

My throat tightens for a second. I suddenly feel like they're all humoring me. Like they're all talking behind the scenes, on their own, and they don't really need me but they're involving me to be nice, because they feel bad for me, because I'm just a kid.

My throat tightens even more. I don't like this.

"I'm always free. I mean, not always. Not during school. But I could skip school!" I say, like I'm in control and make my own decisions all the time. I feel Anna and Cybil looking at me, probably making eyes at each other about how dumb I sound. My face turns hot and I clench my teeth.

I really don't like this feeling.

"Okay, well, we want you to be there. Let's plan for tomorrow after school."

"Great." I perk up a little. "I'll tell Cybil. She's right here."

"Wonderful. I think Doug is going to join as well to show the website." She pauses for a moment. "This is all coming together, Ellie!"

The way she says it, I feel like I'm forced to believe her, like there's no other choice, but then my stomach sinks a little. Is it definitely coming together? What if my grandparents and parents change their mind? What if this restaurant developer's offer is too good to pass up?

I mean, there are a million what ifs.

I don't like what ifs. I like *guaranteed* ifs.

Chapter 17

Eleanor Talia Glantz's
GOALS JOURNAL
- Realize that worrying never helps
- Focus on things I can control
- Drink more water

Things get delayed at the hospital and it takes way longer than expected for all the paperwork to be filled out for Bubbie to come home. The waiting makes me anxious. Of course it does, because most things make me anxious. But even without that, I always assume that if something takes a long time, it's going in a bad direction.

Anna and Cybil leave the deli a little bit before us so they can finish a science project. Zeyda is literally locking up the deli for the night when we see Norman. He's right there, through the glass. Does he not understand that this isn't a twenty-four-hour diner? I mean, we're a deli. We have to close sometimes. People don't eat brisket sandwiches at two in the morning. Or do they? Maybe they do! Maybe we should be twenty-four-hours. That concert hall is opening so people will be out late, and they'll be hungry, and they'll need to eat, of course.

I'll discuss this with Zeyda on the ride home. I know he doesn't make the decisions but he's always open to hearing my ideas. That's one of the millions of reasons I love him so much.

"Norman!" Zeyda says, excited sounding for someone who was just about to close and go home for the night and see his wife who's been in the hospital.

"Oh, you're closing up?" Norman asks, like it's not so obvious with the lights off and Zeyda clearly holding a key.

"Well, we can stick around for a minute or two." Zeyda smiles. "What's the latest?"

Norman looks over at me, like kind of asking with his eyes if he should bring this up right now, in front of Zeyda, so I talk back with my eyebrows saying yeah, it's okay for him to bring it up.

I hope he understands what I'm saying.

He hesitates a moment or two longer and then says, "Well, I did some research on the minyan and all the synagogues love the idea. Ansche Chesed suggested someone who is technologically savvy could set up a broadcast on their phone, actually, which is also lovely, because people can't always schlep over. You know?"

"Oh, I know. So much schlepping." Zeyda laughs in a way that says he has no idea what's going on right now but he's here for the experience.

"So much schlepping," I repeat. "Schlepping" is one of my favorite Yiddish words that basically means to haul things and go on a difficult journey.

"I apologize for coming so late. Got caught up on a call with my son. All these questions. Interest rates, mortgages, inspections. Made my head spin." He smiles. "But don't worry about all of that. The synagogues are going to post the minyan information on their websites. I'm happy to be the minyan leader until someone doesn't like how I'm doing it and wants to take over." He chuckles a deep chuckle. "And people can sit and schmooze, buy some nosh, be together. It'll be wonderful."

"I have to admit I don't know anything about this." Zeyda shrugs. "You know Harriet and Mara are the ones in charge here; I just do what I'm told. But if they're okay with it, I'm okay with it."

"Zeyda, I'll explain it all to you on the ride home." I put an arm over his shoulder. "Don't worry."

Zeyda laughs. "Can you believe this? She's only eleven. First woman president I'd say, but we better have a woman in that White House before Ellie is thirty-five!"

Norman nods. "I agree with that. So, I'll let you two get home, and I'll see you here tomorrow around six."

"Drive safe, Norm."

"You, too."

On the ride home, I tell Zeyda a little more about the minyan. He's interested, but then he turns on some news radio station. Sometimes he comments about what he's hearing, and we discuss a little, but we never end up talking about deep stuff the way Bubbie and I do.

Zeyda and I just have a different relationship.

At a red light, he looks over at me and then opens his mouth to say something but stops himself.

It's true that he's really not in charge of things—at the deli, or at home, or anywhere. He's just the quiet, happy, content one who makes everything feel lighter and easier, telling jokes, humming, stuff like that.

"I'm gonna run home to Bubbie," he says when he pulls into my driveway. "Well, not run. Drive. But I'm just so excited to see her!"

They've been married over fifty years and I swear they act like such lovebirds, even now. I hope I'm like that when I get married one day. Mom and Dad love each other, too, but Bubbie and Zeyda are different. They have like a movie star kind of love going on.

"Of course. Give her a kiss for me," I say. "Love ya."

"Love ya, too!" he sings.

I close the car door, walk inside the house, and remember that even with everything else going on, I have a Halloween costume to figure out. That's the "focus on being eleven" part of things.

I quickly say hi to my parents and run up the stairs.

"Aves," I say as soon as she answers my video call. "So okay, I've been distracted with Bubbie in the hospital and all this deli stuff. But update me on Halloween. What's going on?"

She sighs. "For some reason, Sally has this vision that we should all be like, nineties pop stars. She's suddenly obsessed with the nineties."

"She is?"

"Yeah, but the rest of us aren't. I mean, aside from me watching *Friends* a zillion times." Ava sneezes and blows her nose, and it's weird because it's like right into her phone. "Anyway, we're going to finalize at lunch tomorrow. Also, we need to start thinking about outfits for Nina's party."

"So much to do." I giggle.

Ava yawns. "'Kay, gotta finish that math worksheet and go to bed. See you tomorrow, El."

"Nighty-night."

We hang up the call and I get in my pajamas, brush my teeth, and crawl into bed, snuggling up under my covers.

I fall asleep thinking about happy things like the deli still being ours, and the new website, and coming up with an amazing Halloween costume, too.

CHALLAH

INGREDIENTS
2 packs active dry yeast
½ cup warm water
½ cup room temperature water
½ cup and 1 pinch sugar
1 tablespoon course salt
3 eggs
3½ cups flour
½ cup oil

INSTRUCTIONS

1. Mix the yeast, warm water, and a pinch of sugar. Let sit for 10 minutes or until the yeast is activated (the yeast will froth when activated).

2. Add the room temperature water, the salt, the half cup of sugar, and 2 eggs.

3. Beat the mixture for a few minutes.

4. While beating, gradually add 3 cups of flour.

5. Add the oil and last cup and a half of flour.

6. Beat a few minutes more. Then change from beaters to dough hook.

7. Add enough flour to clean the bowl.

8. Move the dough to a warm greased bowl.

INSTRUCTIONS CONTINUED

9. Fill a large sheet pan with hot water and put on the bottom shelf of an oven.

10. Put dough in a bowl on the upper shelf of an oven. Let rise for 90 minutes, punching down halfway through.

11. Turn the dough out on a floured clean surface. If making a six-strand braid, separate the dough into six balls and roll each out into six strands where the tops of the strands come together and the bottoms spread out in a triangle.

12. Then braid in this cadence until a full braid is made. Outside right over two. Second from the left all the way right. Outside left over two. Second from the right, all the way left.

13. When the braid is complete, tuck the ends underneath the loaf, and put the loaf on a greased cookie sheet.

14. Beat one egg with two teaspoons of water. Brush the top of the braid.

15. Refill the pan at the bottom of the oven with hot water and let the loaf rise in the oven for 30 minutes.

16. Brush the braid again with egg wash and let rise for another 30 minutes out of the oven.

17. Preheat the oven to 350 degrees.

18. After the rise is complete, bake for 60 to 70 minutes, or until the loaf is a golden brown.

19. Cool completely.

Chapter 18

At school the next day, Ms. Tomasso has the word STRENGTH on the board. I'm supposed to be writing, but it feels kind of impossible to get started.

"Ellie," Ms. Tomasso calls out from her desk at the front of the room. "You all right over there?"

"Mm-hmm," I reply.

"Okay, well, I don't see your pencil moving." She raises her eyebrows from across the classroom and then goes back to her laptop.

Grrrr. Why is Ms. Tomasso the meanest? With everything else going on, this was a year I really could have used only awesome, kind, patient, nice teachers.

Strength is the ability to do things even when they're hard. Strength is showing up for people and asking the hard questions and waiting for answers, not just waiting to talk. Strength is listening and being there for people. Strength is trying as hard as you can.

"Okay, pencils down, children."

I wish she wouldn't call us children. We're in middle school now. Can't she think of another word for us? I wish. I wonder why it feels so nice when Bubbie says it, but so annoying and condescending when Ms. Tomasso does.

At lunch, Nina's the first one at the table. She's wearing a ripped hoodie, a fancy one that she bought ripped like that, and I'm instantly so jealous. My mom is really not into buying already ripped clothes, even though she understands it's a thing and people do it all the time and the clothes are supposed to be ripped.

She still won't do it, though.

"Hey." I sit down and immediately start unpacking my brown paper lunch bag.

"Ellie!" Nina says, all excited. "How are you?"

"I'm fine, you? Actually, I'm starving. I'm really excited for this mozzarella tomato sandwich my mom made me."

"Yum. That sounds so good." She opens a reusable lunch bag. "I have this chopped salad leftover from dinner last night. Your lunch looks way better."

I smile. "Chopped salad is good, too." I take a bite and finish chewing before I start talking again. "So, what's the latest with your party planning? It's getting closer and I'm excited."

"Everyone's going nuts about it, but I feel like you're all gonna be disappointed." She eats a forkful of salad. "I mean, there's a DJ and stuff, and probably one of those glitter tattoo artists, passed hors d'oeuvres, and then a sushi chef, but that's really it." She pauses. "Oh, and one of those exploding candy cakes."

"Nina!" My eyes are open as wide as they can possibly be. "That's like a bat mitzvah. How does that not seem so great to you?"

She shrugs. "I dunno. It's just how we do parties."

I stare at her for a minute and wonder if she's kidding, or if she's bragging, or if she honestly doesn't think any of this is over the top. It's been a month of school with Nina here and I still don't totally understand her.

Soon the others come in. Aanya is crying about a bad grade on a math test and Brynn is trying to comfort her. This is their dynamic. Usually one of them is crying and the other one is doing the comforting.

Ava sits down next to me and unwraps her turkey sandwich. "Okay, we are finalizing Halloween today. And Nina's party, so we have a lot to plan and organize and discuss," Ava starts.

"Guys," Nina interrupts. "Chill with my party. You're all acting like you've never been to a party before!"

I look over at Ava and her cheeks are bright red. My insides start to feel like sandpaper. I don't like it when Ava gets her feelings hurt. It's almost as bad as when I get mine hurt—maybe worse, actually, now that I think about it, because I'm not in Ava's head, so I can't calm her down the way I do with myself.

"Well, you do go on and on about it," Sally answers. "So obviously we're going to be excited."

Good. I'm glad Sally spoke up.

Nina shrugs.

Aanya and Brynn start cracking up, like the whole thing is really, really funny, while Ava, Sally, and I just sit here kind of awkwardly. I'm glad Aanya is laughing, though, because it seems to take her mind off of the bad grade.

"Moving on." Ava folds her hands on the table. "Are we doing a group costume this year? Nineties? We don't have to."

"Do you guys always do a group costume?" Nina asks. She digs around the bottom of her bowl of salad; I think she's searching for stray pieces of avocado.

"Not always," Ava answers. "A lot, though."

"I think most years," Brynn adds.

"Yeah," Aanya jumps in. "Except third grade when we all got pink eye and had to stay home. Remember that?"

"The saddest Halloween ever," I answer.

"Is everyone in for a group costume?" Ava asks. "Because if so, I have a better, even more brilliant idea that's not only fun, but will also help Ellie's entire family!"

"Oooh, please tell me. I am in! I love the Glantz fam." Sally smiles. "That kind of sounds like a family celebrity band, doesn't it?"

I smile. "Um, kind of."

"Anyway, I'm thinking we all go as pickles! And we can have little signs that say *Eat at Lukshen.*" Ava claps her hands.

I feel shocked, kind of, like not able to believe that Ava would suggest this for some reason. I don't know why—she's always going out of her way for me, but in this moment, it feels over-the-top kind and generous. Like she'd devote her whole Halloween costume experience to help me.

That's love.

"I love pickles," Aanya adds. "And that's pretty funny. So, count me in. Maybe I could even be an okra since it kind of looks like a pickle with a Taste of India sign. Bhindi masala is one of my favorite dishes there and we can have a little restaurant team-up."

Brynn smiles. "This is brilliant."

"Nina?" Ava looks over at her, and I don't know why, but I can tell Ava's enthusiasm about Nina has faded.

"I'm in. I don't know anything about Lukshen or Taste of India, but they sound good." She picks a stray piece of corn out of her salad bowl.

Something about Nina seems a little off today, like she's not talking as much as she normally does.

But at least we have a Halloween plan.

That's something.

Chapter 19

Eleanor Talia Glantz's
GOALS JOURNAL

- Think positively
- Cherish every second with Bubbie and Zeyda
- Try to stop clenching my teeth

Lukshen Loyalty and the community minyan officially start tonight, and I have no idea what to expect. Thirty people could show up and it would be great or two people could show up and we won't have enough for a minyan. Really, anything can happen.

I'm at the deli with Zeyda. Bubbie is doing better but she's still resting at home most of the time. The deli feels empty without her here—lonely, almost. Like even the tables miss her. It doesn't smell the same either—the brisket aroma isn't as sweet, and the fries don't smell as good.

I need Bubbie back here. I need to crunch half sour pickles and hear her call me Ellie-doll.

I walk over to the soup.

Please let Bubbie get back to the deli. Please let me have more time with her here. Please, masterful broth, please.

"So, we don't need to put out food or anything," I tell Zeyda. "The goal is for people to *buy* food. And community, of course."

Zeyda laughs. "Well, people are always hungry. I'll put out some pickles and coleslaw the way we always do when people come to eat here. And they'll probably still be hungry, so then they can order food."

"Good plan."

I stand by the door and wait for people to come, anxious feelings swirling all around my stomach. Maybe this was a bad idea. Maybe people don't want to go out at night. I don't want Norman to feel worse than he already does. I mean, first he loses his wife—what if this community minyan falls flat?

No, no, no. I don't want that.

I stay by the door a while, but then that only makes me more nervous. I keep looking through the glass and then looking away and then looking through the glass again.

Finally, I can't take it anymore. I need to leave this spot.

I start pacing around the deli, organizing the shelves where we have the potato chips and the six-packs of warm soda, cans of chicken broth, and bags of onion rolls. It's the grocery section of the deli even though this isn't really a place for grocery shopping. I'm putting a soda in the back when I hear the door chime. Someone is here.

"Hello?" a lady calls out in a squeaky voice. "Is this the right place for minyan? Hello?"

I peek through the shelves to see if Zeyda is going to talk to her first. I kind of hope so.

"Yes, hello, welcome," he says. I walk around and observe from behind the tables. "I have chairs set up and some nosh on the table over there. Help yourself. More people should be coming any minute now."

My throat tightens. Zeyda doesn't know that for sure, and he still doesn't totally seem to understand what's going on. To be honest, I'm a little shocked I'm even allowed to do this with everything going on with Bubbie.

I'm about to walk over to this lady and take my perch by the door again so I can pray silently that more people show up. We need to have at least ten people in total!

Then my phone starts buzzing in my pocket.

I look to see who is calling. Ava! At a time like this.

"Hi, Ellie," she says and launches into a whole thing. "Do you think Nina was weird today? About the costumes?"

"Um, not really. Sort of. Maybe?"

"Okay, that's not an answer. But honestly, I think she's ditching us for the Lanyards."

"Really?" my voice goes high at the end.

The Lanyards are this group of girls who wear handmade bracelets pretty much halfway up both their arms. They don't call themselves the Lanyards, of course. That's just what we call them. We're not in any classes with them this year, so truthfully I haven't been thinking about them so much.

"I mean, she does wear a lot of bracelets," I say in a soft voice, thinking about this theory.

Ava cracks up. "Ellie! I don't think that's why she's ditching us for them. We all know they're the popular group and we also can probably assume that Nina was way popular in her old school." She pauses. "Don't you think?"

"I guess?" I honestly don't have time for this now, and it's just a bad feeling to think that your new friend really wants to be with other friends. Even though Nina's not my favorite person, she is starting to grow on me.

"How can you not care about this?" Ava says. "What if we go to her party and she's not even our friend anymore?"

"I do care, Aves," I whisper. "But this minyan thing is supposed to start in three minutes and the only person here is this squeaky-voiced old lady who is on her third bowl of free coleslaw."

Ava sighs. "Okay, go, we'll figure this out later."

"Don't stress. Promise me you won't stress? I really don't think Nina's ditching us so fast . . . and also, I'm not sure the Lanyards are taking in new members."

"Good point." Ava pauses. "Also, love that *you're* the one telling me not to stress. But okay. Bye."

Zeyda and Squeaky Voice Lady sit and chat for a few more minutes while I stare at the window, waiting for more people to come.

"Ellie-doll!" I hear, coming from the back.

Oh, my goodness. Bubbie. She's here.

I whip around and run to greet her. She looks pale, with dark circles around her eyes, and her hair is flatter than usual since she hasn't been to the beauty parlor (that's what she calls it). And she's walking with a cane, much slower than she usually walks.

But she's here! And she's smiling.

"I didn't know you were coming, Bub." I reach over and hug her, feeling tears piling up behind my eyes. Happy, grateful, relieved tears.

The soup. It heard me.

"I wouldn't miss the first night of your minyan, Ellie-darling." She smiles a soft smile. "Now let me get to a chair and sit down."

I look toward the back again and see my mom walking in, worn out, going right to the office. I have a million questions for her, but I decide to wait to ask any of them.

Bubbie makes it to the table with Squeaky Voice Lady and Zeyda. She smiles at them and asks how they're doing. I get her a glass of ice water with lemon because hydration is so important. Ta-da!

"Helloooo," a lady sings a few minutes later, walking into the deli as the door chime makes its twinkly sound. "Harriet, my love? Where are you? Estelle, Darlene, Mina, and I are here. Harriet, we're so happy you're out of the hospital. We hope you're here, doll."

Wow, this lady talks a lot for someone who is literally just walking into a place. I mean, there could be tables of customers here. I guess she sees that the tables are pretty empty, but wow. She has so much to say.

"Rosie!" Bubbie calls out. Normally she would get up to greet her, but not today. That's okay, though. Baby steps. I can't expect her to be completely better right away. "You made it!"

"Of course I made it." Rosie shakes her head. "My mother lived to be one hundred and two and I still miss her every second of every day. I'd say Kaddish forever for the kind of mother she was." She sniffles. "Anyway, I brought the gals. We're going to order when we're done. That's okay, right? You're not closing early or anything? We're just so thrilled to see you."

"I'm thrilled, too." Bubbie laughs a more tired sounding laugh. It doesn't sound like her. "We'll get whatever you need. Come sit."

The lady, Rosie, sits down, while her train of three older women—who I presume are Estelle, Darlene, and Mina—follow. I finally come out from where I was hiding behind the shelf. I do a quick count. We have Squeaky Voice Lady, plus Rosie and her three friends, Norman, Bubbie, and Zeyda. That's eight. We still need two more. I wish my parents could be here, and Ava's mom and Terri, but there's a meeting at school about the budget, and apparently it's verrrrry important.

With a minute to spare, Norman traipses in with a few friends. We made it to eleven! Eleven people! Okay, it's not like the deli is overflowing for this, but it's only the first night.

"Harriet!" one of the men with Norman says. "Please tell me you have hand-sliced pastrami for me. I've been dreaming about it all day."

"Oh, Ron." Bubbie shakes her head. "I just got out of the hospital, but of course we do! Can you wait until after minyan?"

"It'll be hard, but I'll try." He smiles.

Everyone sits down, munches on pickles, and then Norman starts the service. He has a loud, commanding voice usually, but for this minyan he's sort of quiet and soulful, singing some of

the melodies, reading some thoughtful passages. Then, finally, he asks for people to say the names of their loved ones and then recites the Mourner's Kaddish.

"Norman Blackstein, you should've been a rabbi!" Rosie yells at the end. "You missed your calling, my friend."

"Oh, Rosie." He shakes his head. "I had to take over my father's plumbing business. I didn't have a choice. Maybe in my next life."

"Not too late, Normie," one of Rosie's friends says. "Not too late."

Norman shakes his head again. "You're all too much."

"And I'm too *starving*," the pastrami sandwich guy yells.
"Can we ord-ah some food please?"

"Yes, there's more than enough food." Zeyda smiles. "I'll take your orders here and bring everything out as fast as humanly possible."

"I'll help!" I yell, taking an order pad and a pen off of the counter. "What can I get for you?"

Chapter 20

Eleanor Talia Glantz's
GOALS JOURNAL

- Do homework right away instead of procrastinating
- Volunteer to babysit Mabel more and maybe some kids in the neighborhood
- Make more of an effort ~~initiating~~ plans with friends

"You know, I think it's amazing that you care so much," Anna says to me at breakfast the next morning. "It took me a while to realize it, 'cuz you're my little sister and I feel like there's some rule that I have to find you annoying, but I think you're great."

I look up from my bowl of cereal, my throat burning like I might start to cry all of a sudden. "Anna, wow. Thank you."

"I love you, El."

We finish breakfast and I grab my jacket and backpack and head outside. Ava's already waiting for me, sitting on my front step. I look at my watch.

"Am I late?"

"No," she says, sounding glum. "I was just bored and wanted to leave the house."

"You okay?" I look at her, squinting from the sun in my eyes.

"Yeah, I guess." She stands up and we start walking together. "This Terri thing. It's just weird. Like, she stayed at our house super late last night. I was getting ready for bed, she and my mom were downstairs doing a puzzle together, and it was so strange. I mean, my mom came in and kissed me goodnight and sang the *Golden Girls* theme song like always, but then I just kept thinking of Terri downstairs at our kitchen table while it was all going on."

I nod, unsure of what to say. I obviously have no experience with one of my parents dating someone other than my other parent. I can't really imagine what that would feel like.

"I think it's just a hard adjustment," I say, finally, after listening to the sounds of our sneakers moving along the sidewalk for what felt like too long. "It'll be okay, now you're just in the weird part."

Ava nods. "Yeah, true. Very weird."

"You like Terri though, right?" I ask, even though I know the answer. But I'm just trying to seem open to whatever Ava has to say so she knows I'm here for her.

"I do, yeah," she says softly, so low it's hard to hear. "But, like, will this be the end of the relationship my mom and I had? Like if she marries Terri and stuff? I mean, what will that even be like?"

"Mm-hmm, right." I try not to say too much, so hopefully Ava feels like she can keep talking. I know she'll finish immediately when we get to the bus stop.

Ava pauses. "I don't know. It's all weird. I wish I had a sibling to go through this with."

"That would feel less lonely, I bet." I reach over and drape an arm over Ava's shoulder. "But I'm like a sibling since I'm literally next door. And I'm here for you twenty-four seven."

Ava looks over at me and half smiles. We keep walking to the bus with my arm over her shoulder.

"Anyway, I'm sorry I freaked out about the Nina thing with the Lanyards," Ava says, trying to change the subject, probably because the Terri thing did get kind of intense. "I think she does like us, but I worry she was sort of forced to sit at our table the day she started at school."

I nod. "Yeah, totally. Well, we're the nicest kids in the sixth grade, and everyone knows that."

Ava giggles. "We totally are. I guess that's a good thing. Ms. Tarmesh would never have brought Nina over to the Lanyards' table."

"Never!"

All day at school, I have this ticking clock feeling in the back of my brain. With each day that passes, I'm one day closer to this big restaurant developer meeting, even though I still don't exactly know when it is, and I hate that. I kind of want to just stop time for a bit or stretch it or something.

At lunch, Sally turns to me, lowers her head, and whispers, "So wait, what happens if it's not even your deli by the time we get to Halloween?"

I pause a moment; I hadn't thought of that. "I think it will be. I don't think anything will happen that fast."

Sally shrugs. "Okay, cool. Because, like, I really do want to stand outside Lukshen in a giant pickle costume and hand out candy to little kids."

I laugh. "It sounds fun, right?"

"SO MUCH FUN!"

I've known Sally since preschool. We've always been friends, but never best friends, more like hang-out-in-a-group kind of thing. I don't think we've ever had a sleepover. But she's a constant. A steady. Someone who will always come to your birthday, always write a nice note in your yearbook.

She's reliable and good and right now I really feel grateful for that.

Nina's across the table, smoothing the cream cheese on her cinnamon raisin bagel with a plastic knife, and she just keeps smoothing and smoothing. You can see the knife marks in the cream cheese. It's halfway through lunch and I wonder if she's going to ever actually eat that bagel. It looks so good, though. Better than my already soggy egg salad sandwich, for sure.

"Nina, are you okay?" Aanya asks, putting the cap back on her bottle of iced tea.

She looks up. "Oh, yeah, I'm okay. Just tired." She keeps smoothing the cream cheese.

"You sure?" Brynn asks.

"Yes!" Nina yells. "I'm sure. It's just . . . my sisters are being so rude to me all of a sudden. It's like they're soooo busy and they never have time for me, and my mom is always at the hospital and now my dad is a partner in this firm so he's like working a zillion hours to 'prove himself' or whatever."

I nod. So, she's definitely not okay. I didn't realize how much we had in common before this—I guess it's hard to know what other people are going through if they don't open up about it.

"That sounds hard," Ava replies.

"It is." She looks at all of us. "Anyway, sorry to be a downer at lunch. I know I've been weird the past few days or whatever.

And, like, you're all excited for my party, but now my parents are busy, so who knows if it'll even be cool?"

"I'm sure it'll be cool," Sally says, all excited sounding, talking with her hands.

"Same," Ava adds.

I look over at Ava and wonder if she's going to start talking about what's going on with her, kind of like a commiserating-with-Nina thing.

She opens her mouth to speak but then the words don't come out. Maybe she's scared. Maybe she wants it to be more of a one-on-one thing. Hard to say.

We all try to cheer Nina up for the rest of lunch and reassure her the party will be awesome and all of that, but there's sort of a floating cloud of weirdness in the air. Like we're saying the words to each other but I'm not totally sure we're connecting or making her feel any better.

After school, Ava and I walk to the bus together.

"The deli delivery starts today, right?" Ava asks me. "That's what Terri was saying. I think you're up on the platform and stuff, and she's going to boost it on social media."

"I love how you have this inside scoop." I turn to her and smile. "You kind of know more than I do."

Ava laughs. "I guess it's a silver lining to the weirdness."

"Totally."

We're quiet then and all I can focus on is each of our steps on the gravel as we walk to the bus. Ava and I are never ever quiet together, but there are so many lingering thoughts in our brains. I feel like I'm constantly bouncing from one thought to another, like the space between is some kind of hot lava that I can't settle on.

"I have to tell you something," Ava says suddenly, stopping abruptly right before we get on the bus.

My heart pounds. I don't like the sound of this. Is she switching to the Lanyards' table? Does she not want to be a pickle for Halloween?

Maybe both?

I don't know.

I wish I knew.

"What?" I ask. It feels like my heart could literally jump up from my chest and out of my mouth right now. That's how fast and furious it's beating.

I try to take deep breaths and calm it down.

"So, Nina's dad . . ." her voice trails off.

"Yeah?"

"You know how he's a partner in that firm, but she doesn't say what he does?" Ava asks.

"Uh-huh." I don't know how to tell her that I don't care so much about what Nina's dad does, but Ava is still kind of obsessed with Nina, so I guess it makes sense that she cares.

"And you know how Nina has seemed really weird lately?"

"Yeah . . ."

She shuffles her feet on the gravel for a second and then looks at me with wide eyes. "Her dad is the restaurant developer. The one trying to buy Lukshen. I mean, not alone, I guess. But he's part of it."

"Wait. What?"

Ava nods. "Yeah, they moved here because her dad revitalized this whole area in Chicago, and he was sort of recruited to come revitalize Marlborough Lake."

I'm speechless. I just honestly can't believe this. We've been sitting together and talking about all this other stuff, and *Nina's dad* is behind it? I mean, I know that's his job and it's not personal. But still. I've been working so hard to save it while he's been working so hard to take it away.

"How did you find out?"

Ava sighs. "Well, I video-called her last night to see what was up because she was acting weird, and then it sort of just trickled out. And she feels really bad about it. Honestly, she didn't put it together until I mentioned the pickle idea for Halloween."

I scrunch up my face. "But I talk about the deli all the time."

"But never by name. Maybe she thought there were a lot of delis here? She feels so bad about it. And she's scared to tell you." Ava goes on, "I mean, like, he can still do all the stuff for the other restaurants and restaurant row. Just because Lukshen won't be a part of it, doesn't mean his whole job is pointless. Right?"

"I mean, I don't know. Probably not?" I start to realize that I have no idea what I'm talking about. Maybe I *am* in over my head with this rebrand and trying to save the deli. And then I start to wonder if all the adults are just humoring me, and this is all so dumb and a waste of time.

"Anyway, now it's awkward." Ava shakes her head. "Let's get on the bus. I wish I didn't know this, though."

"Yeah, sometimes too much information is not so helpful."

"Agree."

We shuffle onto the bus and into one of the seats toward the middle. We're quiet most of the ride home.

I can't believe this. I mean, I can. I guess it kind of makes sense, but then I also really can't believe it at the same time.

"So do I, like, pretend I don't know?" I whisper. I'm not sure why I'm whispering since

Nina's not on this bus and everyone else is being really loud and also doesn't know what we're talking about.

Ava rolls out her bottom lip, a thing she does when she's thinking deeply about things. "She did ask me not to tell you . . ."

"But you did tell me . . ."

"I did."

We look at each other with wide eyes and then erupt into laughter because that happens to us sometimes when we're sort of filled to the brim with weird emotions we don't know what to do with.

"What's so funny over there?" Avery Ackerman asks us from across the row.

"Nothing," we answer at the same time.

"Yeah, right. It's never nothing with you two." He shakes his head and turns back to his conversation with Justin Rogovoy.

After that, Ava and I shrug at each other and stay quiet the rest of the ride. My insides turn fizzier and fizzier as the seconds tick by.

I don't know what to do with this information.

I don't want to have it.

I wish I could wipe it away from my brain and not know it anymore.

LUKSHEN (NOODLE) APPLE KUGEL

INGREDIENTS

6 eggs

1 cup sugar

¼ teaspoon salt

½ teaspoon cinnamon

1 cup grated apples (3 apples)

½ cup seedless raisins

5 cups fine-cooked noodles

4 tablespoons melted butter (or margarine)

½ teaspoon vanilla

INSTRUCTIONS

1. Beat the eggs, sugar, salt, and cinnamon together.

2. Stir in the apples, raisins, noodles, butter, and vanilla.

3. Put the mixture into a greased baking dish.

4. Bake at 400 degrees for 40 minutes or until browned.

Chapter 21

fter school, I try to get through my homework quickly because I'm planning to go to the deli for minyan again tonight. I know I don't really count since I'm a kid who hasn't had her bat mitzvah yet, but I still want to be there. Plus, I need to confirm that everyone is all signed up for Lukshen Loyalty.

As soon as I sit down at my desk and take out my notebooks and worksheets, my phone buzzes. It's a text from a number I don't recognize.

> Hey Ellie. It's Nina. Can you talk?

> Um, sure.

A second later, my phone buzzes again with a video call.

"Hi, Ellie." Nina looks sick, like emotionally sick somehow, nervous and pale and not like her usual cool-girl Nina vibe. I don't know what I should say or if I should bring up that I know about her dad and Lukshen. It's weird to know something and then not know if the other person knows you know. Pretty much makes my head spin.

"Hey, Nina." I pause. "You okay?"

She's quiet, her hand over her mouth, and then she bursts into tears, right on this call. She puts the phone down and all I can see is black, but I hear her quiet sobs, like little choking sounds, and then sniffle after sniffle after sniffle.

"Nina?" I ask.

More sobbing. More sniffling.

I honestly don't know what to do because I can't exactly hang up the call, but I don't want to keep asking if she's okay because clearly she's not okay.

I just sit there and listen to her cry.

Finally, she picks up the phone and I see her face again, all red and swollen. Her eyes look like giant gobstoppers but not in a sugary, sweet appealing way.

"Ellie," she says through a sniffle.

"Yeah?"

"I'm really sorry. I don't know what to do. My dad is the person who is in charge of revamping all those restaurants . . . including Lukshen and Taste of India." She cries again and we start the whole process of her putting the phone down and me only seeing black and then her sobbing and sniffling and sobbing.

"Nina, don't cry. Okay? Please don't cry."

I hate this. My stomach feels like it's full of fresh concrete, the kind you always see those people in orange vests putting along the side of the highway. It's filling up and filling up and soon my throat is going to feel all gravelly, too.

"Nina, it's not your fault. You're not in charge of your dad or his job." I pause. "I mean, not that his job is bad or anything but, like, you have no control over it either way . . ."

I really wish she'd come back to the phone. This is super awkward and I'm not getting any homework done.

"I just feel really bad," she says, sort of looking at the screen, but also sort of not. "You're trying so hard to save the deli and my dad is the one trying to take it from you. I don't want to be in this situation."

I nod. "I get that. But it's also not really up to us. My sister is always telling me I should focus on being a kid. I always hate when she says it, but lately I kinda think she's right."

"I guess, yeah." Nina shrugs. "I've never thought of any of this before, but also in Chicago, I didn't really know anyone at the restaurants he was working with, and I figured they'd be glad to get money and stuff." She pauses. "I never thought about the families who actually own these places, and what they mean to them and stuff."

"Right." I look down at the ground. She seems to say *and stuff* a lot. I never realized that before.

"I'm so sorry, Ellie."

I sit back in my chair and wonder how much longer this conversation can possibly go on. I tap my foot on the carpet, eager to move on from this. "You have nothing to be sorry for, Nina. Really." I smile. "Okay, let's just put this aside and focus on your party and Halloween . . . okay?"

"Okay." She sniffles. "Okay."

We hang up a minute later and I feel like something totally hit me out of nowhere, like I fell and now I need to pick myself up and regroup. I didn't expect Nina to call and be so open about her dad. I also didn't expect her to cry for so long—or that I'd have to be the one to cheer her up.

I want to call Ava and tell her about that whole thing, but I don't have time. I need to finish (or start, I guess) homework so I can be ready when Zeyda comes to pick me up.

Bubbie isn't driving yet, and she's not at the deli all day the way she was before she went to the hospital. She sleeps more than she used to, and her voice always sounds a little weak and rattly. But she's home, and she's doing some stuff, and I have faith she will keep getting better.

I rush through the social studies worksheet and then get started on math, but I cannot focus at all on these problems. It's an introduction to algebra and I still don't understand solving for X. It feels like I'm reading another language entirely, almost like when I first learned to read Hebrew. I try as hard as I can but end up guessing on most of them. Oh well.

I run downstairs to grab a snack and I find Mom at the table picking at some leftover challah.

"What's new, El?" Mom asks, sort of distracted but also calm sounding. "Sorry I've been so focused on this meeting; I feel like I haven't checked in on you so much."

"Ummm, well aside from worrying about the meeting. Homework, I guess." I stop talking. I want to tell her about the pickles thing for Halloween, but I wonder if it's a mistake. I don't want to hear anything negative about the deli, something that will set me off and make me feel like none of my efforts are really worth it. "I better get back to it, actually, before Zeyda comes to pick me up."

I head back upstairs to my room, but Anna stops me before I get there. I hadn't even realized she was home.

"Ellie!" she screams, way too loud for someone standing this close to me. "Cybil's first afternoon as delivery person was AMAZING!!!!"

"Really?" My skin prickles all over with this overwhelming sense of pride, joy, hope, and optimism and a million other really wonderful feelings.

"YES! She had so many orders who tipped nicely . . . and each customer signed up for Lukshen Loyalty. They're excited about a free pastrami or tuna sandwich after ten orders! And get this, since it went so well, Mom and Dad said I can go next time!" She pulls me into the tightest hug possible, so fast that our heads clink together and I have to rub my forehead to make the pain go away. But I don't even mind! Because Anna is excited! And Cybil did a great job! And things are really picking up and moving along!

What a roller coaster emotional afternoon.

Nina sobbing, Mom nervous about the meeting, Anna excited and happy . . . I don't know what to make of this.

Chapter 22

Eleanor Talia Glantz's
GOALS JOURNAL

• Try to see things from other people's point of view when possible and be a good listener all the time
• Learn a new Yiddish word every week
• Empty the dishwasher without being asked
• Practice breathing exercises

"I can't believe it," Ava says on our walk to the bus on Friday. "She told you about her dad being the restaurant developer?"

I nod.

"And she was freaking out?"

"Pretty much, yeah. It's not her fault, so she doesn't need to feel bad." I pause. "But then again, if I were her, I'd feel bad, too."

"You would *totally* feel bad!" Ava yells, and I shush her.

We're quiet for the rest of the walk to the bus, which is really only half a block, but still. I kind of expected Ava would have more to say about Nina. It seems like there are other things on her mind, though. Probably the Terri-and-her-mom thing.

We get onto the bus and smoosh into the seat the way we always do—me by the window and Ava in the aisle—and tune out all the ruckus and commotion. ("Ruckus" and "commotion" are our bus driver's words, not mine.)

"Terri was over really late again last night," Ava says after we're quiet for most of the ride.

"Really?" I turn to face her a little more and put my hands in my pockets, and that's when I realize I've forgotten my phone, but I can't focus on that now. *Must focus on what Ava's saying. Really trying to be a good listener.*

"Yeah, she and my mom were playing Scrabble, and then they came up with this idea that they should write a cookbook together."

"You stayed up that whole time?"

"Eavesdroppers never sleep!"

"Is it really uncomfortable?" I ask, because the question just sort of lands on my brain and then feels a need to escape.

"It's really, really weird." She turns to me, teeth clenched. "Just because it's my mom, you know, it's just weird. I can't explain it."

"I know, because all grown-up love is weird. Even when it's your own parents—it's like you want them to love each other but then also not, like, that much. You know what I mean?"

"Yes. Exactly. So glad you get me and this whole thing."

"It's weird and it may be some variation of weird for a while, but soon, I think the weirdness will cool off a bit."

"I hope so."

"Also, we really say the word *weird* a lot."

"A lot," she replies.

We get off the bus and go to our classes. All throughout the day my mind bounces between Nina's family, and Terri and Ava's mom, and then of course this deadline for the meeting.

Tomorrow.

It's happening tomorrow and I honestly have no idea what Mom and Dad or Bubbie and Zeyda will decide.

Some moments I think that we're making so much progress, like with Cybil and the deliveries and the minyan and Lukshen Loyalty, and now we finally have a website and social media and a way for people to order food. But then other moments I think that they're just placating me (vocabulary word, woo-hoo) and it'll all fall flat tomorrow. The money will be too good, and they won't be able to pass it up.

I'm in the middle of math when Ms. Cuchin, one of the office assistants, knocks on the door and asks to speak to me.

My heart catapults out of my chest, assuming the worst. My skin gets hot and I immediately want to run away from myself and the entire world that I know.

"Ellie, your mom said you left your phone at home, so she called the office; she's picking you up today, so don't take the bus."

I stare at her, unable to speak for a few moments. "Wait. Why?"

"Um, I'm not sure. But she didn't seem overly concerned, if that helps. More matter-of-fact."

"Mmm-hmm. Okay."

She smiles. "It honestly feels like not a big deal."

Ms. Cuchin is super young, like maybe she only graduated high school a few years ago, so she kind of speaks like a teenager, and in this moment, it's really, really comforting.

I go back into math and Ava raises her eyebrows at me.

I lean over toward her desk and whisper, "My mom is picking me up today. I'm not taking the bus." My heart pounds again like it just remembered that I'm nervous. "Not sure what that means. I'm so mad I left my phone at home." I frown.

"It's probably nothing," Ava replies. "But annoying about your phone."

"Girls!" Mrs. McClure calls out from the front of the room. "Please stop talking. Ellie, you had trouble with your homework, remember? You should be paying attention."

My cheeks turn the color of beets and I look down at my desk, unable to make eye contact with my mean math teacher or any of the other kids in the class.

I try to focus on everything she's saying about this pre-algebra stuff but of course I can't.

When I get to lunch, I realize that Nina's absent today.

I ask everyone at the table if she's sick, but no one really knows for sure, and my mind is swirling with too many things at the same time to really talk much. I decide I'll call her later when I have my phone.

After school, Ava walks me out to the pickup area before she heads to the buses.

"Hi, El." Mom smiles, leaning over toward the passenger door. "Hop in. The meeting with the developer got pushed to today, and we waited until afternoon so you can be there."

My mouth hangs open. I can't believe the meeting got pushed ahead, but I also can't believe they waited so that I could be at the meeting!

What does this mean? Good or bad? Somewhere in between? I have no idea.

I pull the door closed, buckle my seatbelt, and stare out the windshield. My teeth are clenched, like my fate is about to be sealed.

I know that sounds dramatic.

But it's the truest explanation of where my thoughts are going right now.

"So, Ellie, my love," Mom starts. "You've heard the news, I guess?"

"Huh?" I look over at her. "What news?"

"About Nina's family . . ."

"Oh. Yeah. I did."

"But you heard her dad is pulling out of the negotiations?"

"Wait. What? No. I didn't know that."

My thoughts are a Ping-Pong ball in a match with professional tennis players and they're moving so fast, back and forth, that I can't even really keep track of them.

"Well, I think that's what's happening," she says. "That's one reason the meeting was moved up. Anyway, I don't want this to interfere with your friendship with Nina, and I also don't want this to make you stressed. We're going to figure it all out."

I nod, unable to speak.

I wonder if that's why Nina was absent today.

Everything feels totally strange.

Mom hands over my phone when we get to the deli. Bubbie and Zeyda are already there. I know this because their car is here, but it also makes sense that they'd be here before us.

There's a sign on the front door that the deli is closed for the afternoon; I guess it would be weird and also impossible for customers to keep coming in and out during the meeting.

We walk inside and three of the smaller deli tables are pushed together, making one long table. It's set up super official looking—like it's in a conference room or something. It has a black tablecloth and pitchers of ice water, fancy sort of wine-looking cups at each seat, and beautifully arranged white flowers in vases. I don't know what type of flowers they are. There are a few sturdy binders in the middle of the table, too, like maybe some sort of game plan for Marlborough Lake's restaurant row?

I'm not sure.

"Um, this looks really official," I say, sort of under my breath, not expecting anyone to hear me.

"It does. It is."

I whip around.

Anna is here! And then Cybil comes out from the bathroom. Cybil is here, too? What's actually going on?

"You look surprised to see me," Anna says.

"Um, I kind of am."

"Why? I'm part of the deli, too. So is Cybil. She's an employee now and Mom and Dad and Bub and Zeyda said we could be here. And Ava's mom is watching Mabel. She's just a little too young for this."

I shrug. "Okay. Well, cool. The more the merrier then. For sure."

"You don't seem excited, Ellie." She rolls her eyes at me, and I feel like she's trying to start a fight. No idea why she'd want to start a fight on such an important day, but that's Anna for you.

"I am excited. But I'm nervous, too."

"Right."

Anna walks away to go meet Cybil in the back and I sort of wander around, straightening some shelves, debating if I should just sit down at the table and wait for others to sit, too. And then I wonder if I should put food out—or ask Bubbie or Mom what the deal is, if they're putting food out.

I look around for them, and it's as if everyone has suddenly disappeared. I head to the back of the deli and the office door is closed. I creep closer, sort of putting my ear out to determine if I hear anything. It's all muffled, though. I hear voices but no specific words.

They better come out soon, though. I can't be the only person out in the main section of the deli, here to greet the official restaurant developer people. And now I have no idea who is even coming. Truthfully, I have no idea what any of this means and I'm starting to regret that I wanted to even be here in the first place.

I walk over to the soup.

Please let this meeting go well. Please let Lukshen still be ours by the end of it. Thank you, masterful brothy powers.

I take my phone out of my pocket to call Ava for moral support, but at that exact moment, three people walk into the deli. Two men and a woman are in suits. They look way too official for Lukshen, too official for Marlborough Lake in general.

It's a very relaxed town. I mean, it's on a lake. So that pretty much demands relaxation.

"Hello, I'm looking for Harriet Einhorn," the lady says. "I'm Rita Ochs, from Blue Moon Restaurant Group."

"Oh, hi, I'm Ellie." I smile and try to make myself talk like a grown-up. "I'll be right back. I'll go get her, I mean."

Okay, so much for talking like a grown-up. I didn't sound like a grown-up at all.

I walk back to knock on the office door, and Anna and Cybil burst out from behind the shelf of chips.

"They're here?" Anna asks, sort of gasping in astonishment for no apparent reason because she knew they were coming.

"Yup. Gotta go get everyone."

As soon as I get to the office door, though, my parents and grandparents come out without me having to knock. I try to study their faces. Are they relaxed, stressed, somewhere in the middle? They're smiling. Their shoulders don't seem raised or clenched or anything.

Zeyda sort of has a spring in his step as he walks toward the long table. Bubbie traipses along with her cane, slow and steady, but much slower than I'd like. She looks sleepy, like she'd much rather be in bed.

Eventually we all sit down, and I feel very official that I'm at this table. I wish I'd known the meeting was happening, though. I wouldn't have worn these baggy jeans and my grey crew neck that says CHILL on it. I'd have worn something fancier, more businesslike. I don't know what that is, exactly. I guess I'd have worn something I usually wear to temple.

Oh well.

"So, I think it's an understatement to say we are very excited to be here with all of you," the lady starts. I already forgot her name. Oh, wait, Rita. Now I remember. "We have been admiring your deli from afar for years. The traditional deli is sort of on the decline in this country. So, now that we have the opportunity to come and revitalize Marlborough Lake's dining scene, with Lukshen being a part of that . . . we are really, really thrilled." She keeps her hands folded on the table and smiles at all of us.

We don't need to be revitalized, though! I scream that in my head, careful my mouth is closed and the words don't just fly out on their own. *We're fine. I'm doing the revitalizing. I mean, thanks to Terri. But we're doing it. We really are.*

"We're open to many different arrangements. As you know, there's a very substantial offer on the table," one of the men says. "We're also open to negotiating. We want it to be clear we aren't planning to take away from the already amazing Lukshen Deli culture and flavor and the role it plays in the community."

I look around to try and gauge everyone's facial expressions. They seem smiley and open to hearing more, but I wonder if this is the kind of thing people say but then down the line, it sort of all falls flat.

How can we know for sure? How can we trust them?

"This is all very lovely," Bubbie jumps in, sounding weak. She looks over at my mom. "Mara?"

My mom starts talking. "As you know, Lukshen has been in our family for four generations . . ."

Bubbie interrupts her. "This deli is my pride and joy, other than my granddaughters. They're my real pride and joy. Two of them are sitting here." She points to Anna first and then to me. "The third is at a friend's house, but she's delightful, too."

My mom breathes in and then breathes out. "Okay, so I think what my mother is saying . . ."

I look over at Bubbie, her eyes wide, like she's forcing them to stay open. Bubbie interrupts again. "I'm sorry, but I need to say this. We don't want to lose any of what we have at Lukshen now. There's no wiggle room. I don't want to sell the deli, and I don't care what number you're offering."

I gasp, loudly. I don't mean to do it, but the sound just sort of tumbles out of the back of my mouth.

"So, let me just jump in here," Rita says and then she clears her throat. "Our goal is to help build on the Lukshen brand and take it to the next level. You can remain a vital part of the operation. We are simply here to amplify that. To expand on all the things that are working."

My mom nods. "That sounds great to me."

Bubbie shoots her a look. "Mara, please, let's wait to respond."

Suddenly, my heart starts pounding and my palms turn sweaty. I have to wipe them against my jeans over and over again.

I want to run over to the soup right now but it's not even simmering because the deli is closed, and I don't even know if there's a pot on the stove or if Bubbie put it back in the fridge.

I need the soup to make a wish but right now there's no soup to wish on, not in front of me, anyway. So instead I picture the pot of soup in my head. I imagine the tiny bubbles of fat and the sound it makes when it boils a little bit. I ty to remember the exact smell—the salty, chicken-y goodness. And I make a wish anyway.

Please don't let us lose our deli. Please let Lukshen still be ours by the end of this meeting.

There's silence at the table for a minute or two after that and everyone looks medium stressed, except Zeyda. He's sipping his water, smiling, taking it all in.

"Here's another option, and I want to make this clear," one of the men says. "We're also prepared to offer you a deal that would pretty much change nothing on your end, just to have Lukshen included in our Marlborough Lake restaurant row revitalization. You will still be the face of Lukshen, make all the decisions, the driving force of the business." He pauses. "All we ask is that our logo be included on materials, and that you participate in the restaurant row planning and implementation."

My head starts to spin as he talks, and I start to tune out most of what he's saying.

Instead, I just look to Bubbie, Zeyda, and then to my mom and dad, and then to Anna and Cybil, who appear to be texting under the table. I glare at them to stop, but they don't notice.

"That sounds reasonable and acceptable to me," Mom says, turning to Dad to weigh in.

"I'd love to see the official offer." He smiles. "But I agree."

It's quiet then and my mom says, "Okay, girls, here's when we get into particulars, and I'd like to keep this to people over the age of eighteen." She folds her hands on the table like Rita and raises her eyebrows at us. "Can the three of you hang in the back office for a bit?"

Anna groans but then Cybil grabs her hand and they get up. I follow them to the back.

"Probably could've expected we'd be kicked out for this part." I shrug.

Anna puts an arm around me, and then we sit down on side-by-side swivel desk chairs.

Cybil pulls up funny videos to show us on her phone, and it distracts me a little bit, but not entirely.

All I really care about right now is what's happening at that meeting.

RUGELACH

INGREDIENTS

1 package active dry yeast
¼ cup lukewarm water
3 cups sifted flour
6 tablespoons sugar
2 eggs
2 sticks melted margarine
1 cup sugar
1 tablespoon cinnamon

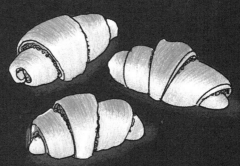

INSTRUCTIONS

1. Combine the yeast and water. Wait until it's all dissolved.

2. Add the flour, sugar, eggs, and margarine.

3. Refrigerate overnight.

4. Roll out the mixture on sugar and cinnamon on wax paper.

5. Cut the dough into eighths and cut each section into eighths.

6. Roll up with the cinnamon and sugar.

Chapter 23

The meeting goes on for another hour or two. Cybil, Anna, and I end up being so starving that we sneak out eventually, take five bags of chips, and eat them faster than I've ever eaten anything in my life.

I guess being nervous also makes you hungry, although it would seem to be the opposite.

Finally, the suited people leave the deli, and Anna, Cybil, and I head out of the office.

"So?" I ask.

"Am I still a Lukshen delivery girl?" Cybil asks.

"Are we billionaires now?" Anna cracks herself up.

Mom smiles. "Yes, Cybil, you're still our delivery girl." She pauses and looks straight into my eyes. "And Ellie, I want you to know, we wouldn't be here if not for you."

"Go Ellie, go Ellie!" Anna sings, and then Cybil joins in.

"Also, I have to say I'm surprised how hungry our minyan-goers are," Zeyda adds. "We have at least ten people every night ordering pastrami and sides! We owe that to Ellie, too."

"So does this mean we're set for life?" I ask.

"Set for life?" my dad repeats. "I don't think so. We still need to build on all the stuff you've started, El. But with this new agreement . . . we're part of the whole plan for Marlborough Lake restaurant row, too."

"And we keep the deli," Bubbie says. "The restaurant group is planning all these events. Their ideas are phenomenal; it's going to be wonderful, wonderful, wonderful. But we keep the deli."

She pulls all of us into a hug, but she's shaky on her feet. My dad gets a chair for her and urges her to sit down.

They all stand around Bubbie, talking, and I stay for a little bit but then I have an overwhelming need to call Ava.

"We did it," I say, as soon as she answers the video call.

"We did what?"

"The deli! It wasn't sold away. It's still ours." I pause. "I mean, we're part of the group and stuff, and who knows what the future holds, but it's still ours."

"That's amazing, El!" She coughs and I hear voices in the background, even though I can't see anyone.

"Wait, who's there? Aside from Mabel?"

She hesitates to answer, and my heart starts to sink a little.
"Oh, um, just Nina, Sally, Brynn, Aanya . . ."

"You mean all of our friends?"

She stalls for a second. "Yeah, but don't worry, we're not leaving you out. You had the meeting today. Don't worry, Ellie."

"I always worry. You know that."

"Come over now," Ava says and the others all pop into the screen, their heads smooshed together. "Get Anna to drive you. We're ordering pizza."

I smile. "Okay, let me go ask."

I walk around to the front of the deli where Anna and Cybil are sitting on the bungee chairs I asked Bubbie to buy last summer. A great addition, I must say!

"Anna, you need to drive me to Ava's. Please. It's important."

"Ask in a nicer way," she says all sugary sweet, imitating a preschool teacher.

"Please, Anna, amazing older sissy of mine, can you please drive me to Ava's house?" I clasp my hands over my heart and smile. "Please. Also, please."

Anna and Cybil make eyes at each other.

"I don't need to start deliveries for another two hours while the deli is still closed," Cybil says. "So, let's do it. And we can drive past the Hackley twins' house on the way back."

"Okay." Anna smiles. "Come on."

I say goodbye and congrats to Mom and Dad and Bubbie and Zeyda and then we all get into the car. Anna blasts some angry-sounding female singer. Cybil and Anna sing together louder than I've ever heard them sing before. It's screechy and laughy but also angry at the same time.

I don't understand them. I don't understand what they're going through. I want to, but I don't.

Finally we get to Ava's and all the girls (minus Mabel, who is watching TV, of course) are waiting on her front lawn for me. It feels nice, like they actually want me there. My left-out feelings get washed away.

"Ellie!" Sally calls out and runs to the parked car. "Sooooo happy you're here."

We all huddle together for a few minutes chatting and discussing pizza toppings. I want pineapple, of course, but Brynn wants mushrooms, and Aanya likes onions and green peppers. Ava and Sally and Nina want plain. It's settled. We'll get three pizzas and there will be leftovers.

Easy.

Nina comes over to me after that. "Hey Ellie, I'm not sure if you heard, but my dad stepped back from the negotiations with Lukshen. That's what he said. I don't totally understand, but anyway, he didn't want to be in the nitty-gritty. Again, his words."

I nod. "Oh, um, yeah, it went fine, though."

"Good." Nina shuffles her feet on the cement for a moment and then looks up at me. "Sometimes this whole thing gets really strange. It starts out as one thing and turns into another. So, anyway, I'm just glad everyone feels good about it."

I stare at her for a moment, feeling confused and shaky, like she's trying to say something without saying it.

"Um, yeah. We do. I think."

"Girls!" Ava calls out to all of us. "Come in the backyard. We need to finish this Halloween plan RIGHT NOW."

We follow her back there, and through the big sliding doors, I see her mom and Terri at the kitchen table, working on a puzzle. Their heads are close together and they're smiling and they seem happy. Really, really happy.

It never occurred to me that you could find love later on in life, that your idea of love could totally change. Life is so confusing to me. I wonder if it'll ever totally make sense.

"Okay, so we're on board with this pickle plan?" Ava asks, stretching her legs out on the lounge chair. It's a brisk fall day but the sun is shining so it feels pretty warm. We're in jeans and hoodies but we're acting like it's still summer.

"I'm definitely in," Sally says. "I love pickles. Can we eat pickles while we're dressed up?"

"Oooh," I say, excited. "That's actually an amazing idea. We could hand out pickles to trick-or-treaters that want those. I mean, we'll have candy, too. Of course we'll have candy!"

Everyone starts laughing and I can't tell if they're laughing at my idea or my insistence on candy. Maybe both.

"Do kids like pickles?" Brynn asks. "I mean, I do. I did as a kid. But it might be weird . . ."

I wobble my head from side to side. "Yeah. Maybe."

I look over at Nina and she's super quiet, playing with all of the bracelets on her wrist.

"Nina, are you okay?" I ask.

She sniffles. "Yeah, I guess." She looks over at each of us. "I still feel wobbly about the whole restaurant thing."

"Nina!" I yell, without meaning to. "It's fine, though. It all worked out. You don't need to feel wobbly! Feel un-wobbly!"

"My family seems happy with their offer too, Nina," Aanya says. "I'm not as close to my cousins' restaurant as Ellie is to her deli, especially since my parents aren't even involved, but I think I heard something about your dad getting free garlic naan for life for his contributions. So really, don't sweat it. The restaurant group is scary, but your dad is a good guy. Like Ellie said, it all worked out."

Nina shakes her head. "Yeah, but that's the thing. It feels like it all worked out. But who knows down the line?"

I crinkle my eyebrows in Ava's direction, feeling very confused—I don't understand what Nina's saying and I also don't understand why she's saying it, or what the ultimate goal is. For all the talk about me acting like a kid, she's the one who's really acting like an adult. A very, very nervous adult! Maybe I should talk to her about that pamphlet.

"Let's just pause this whole restaurant developer deli thing," Ava jumps in. "This is grown-up stuff, and as I've been telling my BFF and next-door neighbor Eleanor Talia Glantz, we need to focus more on being kids. I mean, childhood is fleeting . . . we only have so much time to really enjoy it."

"Now you sound like an adult!" Brynn yells. "Also, my mom is picking me up in ten minutes because she has a school board meeting tonight. So can we just decide so we can order the costumes and be done with this?"

"Yes!" I yell. "All in favor of being pickles for this year's Marlborough Lake Halloween parade, say aye!"

"Aye!" everyone shouts at the same time.

"Perfect," Ava says. "Everyone order the costumes tonight, so they come in time. Sooooo excited. And I think there's a deal on this one site that if we order more than three, we get ten percent off. So maybe we should order them all together."

"Amazing." I smile.

We hang in Ava's backyard for a little while longer. After all the girls get picked up, I walk home.

It seems like everything should feel calm and easy-peasy lemon-squeezy, but it doesn't for some reason.

I wonder if it's my brain that won't let me feel that way, or if there's something else to be worried about.

I guess, somehow, there will always be something to worry about, and I need to work on calming down my thoughts, and calming down myself as much as I can.

Chapter 24

The next week pretty much flies by and before I know it, the weekend is here again. Cybil and Jerry are busier than ever with so many delivery orders. It's probably because it's been really rainy and cold all of a sudden. It actually feels like fall now, so I guess people don't want to go out as much to pick up dinner and food for their families.

Every night I go to the deli for minyan even though I don't really need to. It's fully up and running, thanks to Norman. Sometimes Anna and Cybil come, too, which puts us way above the ten people requirement, anyway.

I like to be there, though. I like to see all the people gathering together, chatting, comforting one another even though they're all going through a hard time. Also, let's be honest. I like the food. I like how Bubbie puts out miniature versions of all their different sandwiches. I like sipping the bottled cream soda. I like all of it.

I especially like the ride home with Bubbie and Zeyda. I like that it's dark out and it's cozy in the car with the seat warmers on. Even though Zeyda drives instead of Bubbie now, and I have to sit in the back seat, I like being with them. Sometimes I inch forward during the ride and reach over to grab Bubbie's hand.

I like how Bubbie smells like deli food but also perfume and it sounds gross but it's actually the perfect combination. I like that Bubbie has the energy to put perfume on again.

"Oh, my Ellie," Bubbie says, holding my hand for what actually feels like a very long time. "You're so delicious."

I smile. "Bub, you always say that."

"Well, it's true."

"Do you think you call people delicious because you work in food service or just because, like, you'd call people delicious anyway, because it's one of your words?" I ask her.

She chuckles. "I'm not sure. But very interesting question! I'll think about it."

"Let me know what you come up with." I turn down my butt warmer a little bit because sometimes they really do get too hot. "How are you feeling, Bub?"

"I feel tired but good," she says, so fast it's like she didn't even have to think about it. "I am trying to just appreciate each day and not worry too much about the future."

I pause for a moment and take that in. "Seems like a smart plan."

"I'm happy about this new direction for the deli. I'm happy to be part of this revitalization of Marlborough Lake. I love this town and it's been sad to see the Jewish community declining . . . I know we're really only talking about revitalizing restaurant row, but it's a start." She pauses. "I feel hopeful. Optimistic."

"Me, too. For sure."

We're quiet for a little while and Zeyda turns up the music—Carole King—their favorite. We all sing along to "Tapestry," and I wonder if I'm the only eleven-year-old in the world who knows this song.

I wonder a lot about myself as an eleven-year-old, since I don't always feel eleven. And then I wonder what that even means, to feel a certain age. Like if anyone ever feels their age.

It makes me sleepy to think about, actually.

Like it's a thing I don't need to really wonder about at all. I need to just be.

We get to my house. I lean forward and give Bubbie and Zeyda kisses on the cheek, and then hop out of the car.

Through the big bay window in the den, I see my whole family sprawled out on the couch, watching some show and digging their hands into an overflowing bowl of popcorn. I don't know what they're watching but it must be funny. Even Anna is laughing.

I pause a moment and just watch them through the window, and it fills me with warm feelings. Soon I'll be inside, nestled between Mom and Dad, eating popcorn, too.

Things are good. I have a family who loves each other and good friends and a cozy warm bed to sleep in every night. Bubbie's health seems stable, hopefully even improving. The deli is still ours and it's actually thriving now.

It took a lot of twists and turns and ups and downs to get here, and I guess none of us really know what the future holds. No matter how much we want to, we just can't.

All I know for sure is that right now, this minute, things are good.

BLINTZ SOUFFLE

INGREDIENTS

¼ stick butter or margarine

2 packages of blintzes

4 eggs

1½ cups sour cream

¼ cup sugar

2 teaspoons vanilla

1 teaspoon lemon juice

INSTRUCTIONS

1. Spread the butter or margarine on a glass dish.

2. Place the blintzes on top.

3. Mix the rest of the ingredients.

4. Pour the mixture over the blintzes.

5. Bake at 350 degrees for 45 minutes.

Chapter 25

It's finally the day of Nina's party. I'm having a late lunch of some leftover blintz souffle and a can of seltzer when I realize something.

I actually, finally feel like I can be eleven. Really and truly.

The deli stuff is settled, Anna and I are getting along, and Bubbie's health is stable. At this exact minute, all my brain is thinking about is that I have an amazing, fun birthday party to go to.

You can't get much more "be eleven" than that, but then again, maybe thinking about being eleven is actually not being eleven at all.

My head starts spinning and I decide I need to stop thinking about all of this, actually.

After lunch, I go over to Ava's so we can get ready together.

"It's not weird we're matching, right?" Ava asks me. We're side-by-side in front of her full-length mirror, admiring ourselves in our smocked skirts and matching tank tops with jean jackets over them.

"I don't think so," I say. "It's not like our outfits are the exact same color."

"True." She smiles. "We look goooood."

"We look verrrrry good."

Ava and I crack up after that, admire ourselves some more, and then we head downstairs so Ava's mom and Terri can drive us to the party.

"Ellie!" Terri says as soon as she sees me. "I keep checking the Lukshen Loyalty stats on the website and you're on fire, girl!"

"I am?" I smile. "I mean, okay, I know I am. Someone already came in for their free soup—they filled up the punch card so fast!"

"You're incredible," Ava's mom says.

"And what am I? Chopped liver?" Ava laughs. "No pun intended, 'cuz ya know, deli . . ."

We all crack up. "You're def not chopped liver, although Bubbie's chopped liver is sooo good."

When we get to Nina's party, there are little, twinkly, bright lights all around her backyard, and a DJ is playing fun, boppy dance music.

"You're here!" Nina yelps and pulls Ava and me into a tight hug. "Yay! Thank you SO much for coming."

Aanya, Brynn, and Sally arrive soon after that and then Nina's parents bring out trays of mini hot dogs and little puffed pastry things and there are tall cups of pink lemonade with pink-and-white paper straws.

The DJ plays "Feel This Moment." We all put our arms around each other's shoulders, and we're dancing and scream-singing and for the first time in so long I'm not worrying. Not at all. Not one bit.

I keep singing and dancing and I do what the song says—I stop time and enjoy this moment and then I make a pact with myself. I'm gonna try to do that as much as possible. Actually feel the moment. Not just now, but *all the moments.*

Struggles will come; there will always be stuff to worry about. I can't say I'll never feel anxious again. I know I will.

But that doesn't mean I can't stop and enjoy life, that I can't feel the moments.

I realize now that I don't always need magical soup to make my wishes come true.

Sometimes a change of mindset and a pact with yourself helps, too.

Feel this moment. Be eleven.

I can't wait to see what comes next.